Just Another Saturday Night

Just Another Saturday Night

by
Fionn Murphy & Simon Bramhall

Scalpel Stories

ISBN 978-1-9161915-2-5

Already published in kindle and paperback by Simon Bramhall and Fionn Murphy
Trick or Treat?
Charity: A Dip Into Donation Paradise

Disclaimer
Just Another Saturday Night is a work of fiction. All characters in this publication are fictitious any resemblance to real persons, living or dead, is purely coincidental.

www.scalpelstories.com

Dedication

This book is dedicated to Healthcare workers the world over

Contents

Chapter One

It was a woman's voice. Tracy fought back.

"And your point is?" she said, emotionless – always the best way.

"You sprained your wrist on Tuesday and now you need emergency treatment? At…" she glanced at the clock "Eight o'clock on a Saturday evening? Four days after the event." Tracy hoped the dramatic pause that followed would have an effect, but she was wrong. Again.

"Does it hurt? … Not really but you're first reserve for the ladies darts tonight …. Are you left-handed? … There's no problem then, is there? …. Well, our current waiting time is…" she winced at the writing on the wall in the waiting room, "… between four and five hours, unless you're an emergency. Which you are not." End of. She put the phone down.

Her sigh extended out into the waiting room and circled languidly, looking for somewhere to roost. But all the chairs were occupied, even the one with the deformed leg. It's occupant, an impossibly slender woman with eyes hidden behind celebrity status aviators had perched herself at the stable side of the seat and was precariously balanced at an angle designed to counter the deformity and to achieve balance. As long as she did not move it would work. Tracy could not remember exactly what the woman had said she had come in for – something euphemistic that a receptionist was not supposed to understand. Certainly not for the dazzling sunlight, she had remarked. It had seemed like a joke but it wasn't, as they both knew. But the woman was not in apparent distress or bleeding over anything so that would have to do. On her face, what was left of it outside the sunglasses, she wore the same expression as the rest of the assembled throng, something between resignation and forlorn hope, carpeted with resentful endurance,

It was quiet. Everyone had been listening to Tracy's telephone conversation. Nothing else to do. Ears on Tracy but all eyes on the door to the Holy Grail: the treatment and assessment room. It was shut. They had given up watching the red digital writing on the wall, revolving relentlessly round and round the information screen on an eternal loop going nowhere, repeatedly urging them to try their pharmacist or GP for non-emergency conditions. Duh. They were emergencies, obviously – why else were they here?

The phone rang again and Tracy gave it the obligatory three rings before she picked up the receiver. Never answer the first ring – too keen. Let it ring again to make sure it's really happening and answer on the third. Not the fourth, mustn't keep the clients waiting; any more than three rings and it gives the wrong impression; makes them think we're inefficient and we can't have that, can we? Or, even worse, uncaring. Why the hell not Tracy wanted to say, but not to her line manager. She said it often enough at home though, by way of compensation. Therapy even.

"Wyeminster NHS Trust Emergency Department. I'm Tracy. How may I help?" Tell me something I don't know, following the script written and laid down by the aforementioned Trust, word perfect, never changing; wtf in every syllable, just another Saturday night.

There was a silence. Tracy's goose-flesh chicken-plucked eyebrows launched themselves into her forehead and every eye in the waiting room eagerly watched their ascent. Something happening at last! Anticipation clutched bowels, teeth clenched, breath was held, hopes rose.

"You want to know if your canary is an emergency? ... It's not moving and there's no mist on its mirror." Human breathing resumed, wholesale, noisily and joyously as the audience settled back to enjoy themselves."If it's dead then no amount of mouth to beak is going to bring it back. I suggest you contact the RSPCA. Or maybe St Francis … Try a séance. Thank you for calling the Wyeminster hospital, working for the very best in patient care."The receiver squeaked as it hit the cradle which winced in pain and vibrated indignantly. Tracy's eyebrows returned to base, heavily pencilled, as dark as the roots of her brittle psychedelic badger print hair. And yes, she knew it needed washing which was why it was tied back, wasn't it? Not her fault if she had to work another effing late weekend shift because madam almighty who was supposed to do it had bailed on grounds of ill health. Who didn't get migraines? Tracy had fibromyalgia but no one ever heard her complain, not even when she was in agony, when she was exhausted, could barely pick up the phone let alone manoeuvre the computer mouse sticky with other people's DNA. Sometimes the pain was an ache, occasionally it was like being stabbed and there were even times when she felt she was burning, immolating from within. What was for certain was that the pain was always there, like the weather and the patients and her past. Sitting at reception, susceptible to draughts, infection, obliged to rely on an NHS issue non-swivel, non-ergonomic, non-friendly chair it was little wonder that her neck and back ached with the kind of remorseless fervour of Flat Earthers. She did not sleep properly at night but did that mean she was qualified for night reception duty? Oh no. The fatigue was akin to having flu, her muscles went into spasms from sitting and then there was the fibro-fog. It was absolutely not her fault that she forgot the occasional small detail. The glitches in the computer system could never be placed at her door – way beyond her pay scale – and the Wyeminster NHS Trust should think themselves lucky to have her, someone of her experience, quality and finesse. She shifted her buttocks uneasily on the narrow chair seat and uncrossed her legs, remembering what she had read about varicose veins. Cross legs at the ankle was what the article had said, but then she could not fit all of her bottom on the chair and was liable to slide off it. Perhaps if she rested her feet against the counter for support … but then she could not reach the computer although the phone could be shifted a little closer. If she could be bothered to move it.

Another Tracy-sized sigh launched itself into the waiting room and was all set to follow its orbital path when it was intercepted and blocked: mission aborted. A foreign body stood on the other side of the reception area.

"Yes?" Tracy spoke.

It replied.

"Excuse me, but I've been waiting for over 45 minutes and still haven't been treated."

Every ear, and all eyes now on Tracy, public enemy number one, being challenged by one of their own!

"Have you been assessed by the triage nurse?"

"Half an hour ago."

"Can you read?"

A corporate intake of breath but reluctant recognition that Tracy had assumed the advantage. How would the patient respond? Feebly, apparently.

"Sorry?"

"The big screen over there on the wall. With writing on it. What does it say?"

All heads turned obediently to study the digital screen on the wall, the one with the endless loop of irrelevant information.

"But that's the waiting time for non-urgent cases."

A suppressed groan of despair throughout the waiting room; he had walked right into it. Now all she had to do was wipe the shabby lino floor with him. But Tracy was going to make him suffer first.

"And your point is?"

There was disappointment at the receptionist's response – something more original would have been nice but, well, she was only a receptionist.

"Obviously I'm an urgent case. I'm in unbearable pain. I can't hardly speak or stand it hurts so much. Breathing is agony. It's a miracle I haven't already collapsed – it's only a matter of time before I do. Look! Look at my thumb! Hanging on by a thread. Look at the blood!"

"It's not bleeding."

"But it was. Everywhere. All over my car when I was driving. It's stopped now or I'd have needed a transfusion."

"It looks firmly enough attached to me."

Tracy was right, the room had to concede even though their sympathies were with the victim. There but for the grace of and all that. But he had guts, you had to hand it to him. And he was not going down without a fight.

"You're only the receptionist so what do you know? I need to see a doctor. Now! I have my rights!"

"So do I, love, much good it does me. I'm in constant agony and I work here. Fibromyalgia if you know what that is. Now that's pain. Can't sleep, ache everywhere, swollen hands and feet. You have no idea what I suffer but do you hear me complaining?"

"What about the Patient's Charter and government target waiting times?"

"Like you said, love, I'm the receptionist, not the Minister for Health. They're targets. There's magazines on the table, or there were…" she surveyed her audience with an accusatory stare. Those with magazines winced and pretended to read. "There's a coffee machine in the corridor. You've been assessed, you're in the system and it takes as long as it takes."

The man with the thumb slunk back to his seat which was now occupied by someone else. So he sat on the floor, leaning against the wall below the mocking screen and ostentatiously examined his injury. Perhaps if he wiggled it a bit the bleeding would start again but what if it did and he wasn't seen quickly? It was a sobering thought and he decided to leave it alone but to breathe as heavily and painfully as his crouched squat on the lino permitted.

"Oi! I've been waiting longer than him! What about me? No one knows more about pain than me. Day in, day out, never without it. Constant agony is my second name."

Salvation! God moves in mysterious ways. The Man with the Thumb forgot about his pain and perked up no end – an ally, of sorts. Divine intervention in the form of a fat lady on a plastic chair who was taking on Tracy the Receptionist with all the vigour and strength that he had failed to find. Nemesis also appeared to have back up in the form of another, arguably less fat lady sitting beside her, wearing pendulous earrings.

"Yeah. Me too. That's not fair. What about the queue? Why can't he wait like the rest of us? We've been here longer than him and you don't hear us complaining, do you?" It was thrown out into the room and Thumb Man looked suitably ashamed, bowed his head and sniffed an apology. But he need not have worried. Nemesis's sidekick had moved on – he was but a tool with which to do battle: collateral damage. A casualty of war.

Pendulous Earrings addressed Nemesis.

"You were here before me and I've been here hours." And at that moment an alliance was formed; formidable, determined, united. They introduced themselves: Pendulous Earrings rejoiced in the name of Shazza, Nemesis the somewhat less Olympian, Dawn

Tracy retaliated immediately in an attempt to disarm and undermine, but size was on their side.

"It hasn't been hours. And it's names."

"Yer what?"

"Constant agony is two words, not one, so it can't be your second name. It has to be names."

"It might be hyphenated" an anonymous wit offered from an unidentified location but then relapsed into silence under the steely glare of She behind the reception desk.

"Cheeky mare" Shazza of the dangly earrings announced to tacit general approval and Dawn the avenging angel resumed her crusade.

"Who does she think she is?"

Alas, that would never be known because at that moment the phone rang and Tracy was obliged to reconnoitre elsewhere in order to answer it. On the third ring, precisely, she lifted the receiver as the double doors at the department entrance crashed open. The doors were automatic, designed to open at the first step of the tread on their hallowed portals but this was different somehow – important. Significant. As soon as the woman with the boy in the wheelchair with the squeaky wheel entered the waiting room, it became obvious why.

The lady was robust, in every sense, but not in a jolly way. No one messed with Her. She stormed into the room, pushing the protesting wheelchair ahead of her as a chariot; Boadicea leading her tribe against the ravaging hordes. The tribe followed, meekly, both of them, loyal to the death because the alternative was too unbearable to contemplate. The boy in the wheelchair was silent, pale, eyes closed and mouth twisted with pain.

"My son! He's got acute appendicitis! If it bursts, he'll get peritonitis and die!"

The room froze, tense with excitement. Tracy was answering the phone. Boadicea parked her chariot in front of the reception counter and assumed position, poised, ready to launch.

Tracy had just reached the 'I'm Tracy, how may I help?' part of the script when Boadicea began her assault. But she had underestimated her opponent. The receptionist shot a contemptuous glance at the invader and continued talking. The room held its breath. The computer screen blinked, the double doors sneaked shut without a murmur, all the better to hear; even the digital noticeboard seemed to pause on its endless journey back to its beginning.

"One moment please. I'll be with you in a minute." Tracy said the words without looking at the woman and resumed her conversation on the phone. A thrill Mexican-waved around the room, which still held its breath. If something did not happen soon, it would be asphyxiated.

"Sorry about that" Tracy said into the phone receiver. "I suggest you ring the NHS helpline and …"

"Put that phone down. Now." Boadicea advanced; confident, assertive. She was not particularly tall, or wide, but she did have presence: lots of it, and all her own. Shoulders back, titanium, she led from the jaw. Boadicea wore Boden dresses, bought new, worn for a year then sold for a profit on eBay, with pearls around neck and in ear lobes. She never wore trousers but liked sensibly heeled boots in which her size 3 feet left size 7 prints.

"Sebastian Rosedale. Eleven. Blood group A positive if he needs a transfusion. Allergic to dairy and gluten; sensitive skin, high temperature, tender abdomen. Feels sick. Call a consultant."

Tracy had heard it all before, too often. But this woman did sound assured, even knowledgeable. It could be straight off Google of course, but the way it had been delivered implied some medical background and the woman definitely had confidence. Nevertheless, no one ever got one over on Tracy and she was not going to let them start now. She stuck to her guns. Emitting a sigh, she turned ever so slightly in her chair, easing her buttocks uncomfortably to one side so as to facilitate the manoeuvre, and insolently fingered the mouse. The computer burped up a new screen.

"His date of birth?"

An IED under a passing military vehicle could not have produced a more explosive response. By now the waiting room and its occupants were breathing freely, loving the excitement. Most were rooting for Sebastian's mother, but the old lags were wiser and knew never to underestimate Tracy. She had form, an impressive track record and years of experience.

Mrs Rosedale, for such was Boadicea's name, hit the volume button.

"For God's sake, woman! Get a consultant before he dies!"

Tracy ignored her. See no evil; hear no evil. Head down; do not draw attention. Both of Mrs Rosedale's accompanying tribe shuffled uncomfortably and shifted uneasily from foot to foot as if preparing to march but not sure with which leg to lead. The older man stared disconsolately at the floor and appeared mesmerised by the lino; the younger one looked earnestly at the moving screen on the wall, reading every word carefully as if to check that it was the same the next time it came around. Dawn shook her chins, let out a howl of glee and squealed,

"He's about to die!"

Having the benefit of front row seats, the two fat ladies were in an enviable position of authority and the news spread instantly around the room. The reaction was immediate. Every sentient person was outraged – he was just a kid, life was so cruel, it was so unfair, why hadn't he been treated, where were the medical profession when you needed them? They had been waiting hours which was bad enough but making a child suffer like that was all wrong; it shouldn't be allowed. What happened when his appendix burst? Would they see anything? How long would it take for him to die? There was some scuffling at the back of the room as people adjusted their seats for a better view; some abandoned their chairs altogether and stood up if they could. The Man with the Thumb suddenly found he was in a position of advantage having been forced to place himself against the wall when he lost his place. Now he could move into pole position and became a commentator on events for those less fortunate, like the Chorus in a Greek tragedy.

It was all terribly exciting. Just like one of those hospital dramas on telly but better because they were in it! Mobiles at the ready, YouTube fame and fortune on the horizon; anything might happen. As the divine Dawn was saying, you never knew what lay around the corner. Except that around this corner lay something far more formidable: the senior sister, doyenne of the department who carried almost all before her on an impressive chest and the rest around her person in the form of too, too solid flesh. Sister Delyth Rees.

She appeared as if from nowhere, a navy-blue presence with white edged sleeves and sturdy black legs. Her arrival was silent and final. Tracy seemed to shrink behind the desk, Thumb Man slithered quietly down the wall to his former recumbent crouch at its base; Dawn and Shazza stared with undisguised awe. Now here was someone who mattered – one of their own. Not as large but akin in size; someone to admire and aspire to. A Force. To be reckoned with.

Sister Delyth surveyed the room, slowly moving her head from one side to the other like an owl waiting for something to move. She missed nothing. Shazza's earrings came to a stop, the skinny lady closed her black eye as if to make it disappear, the deformed chair tried to straighten its leg as all the others stood to rigid attention. Even Mrs Rosedale shuffled uncomfortably as Delyth's gaze came to rest on the Iceni entourage standing by the reception desk. Only Sebastian seemed unmoved; He was white, wore beads of sweat like an embryonic moustache on his upper lip and had his eyes tightly shut. He had his knees bent up to his stomach and was hugging them for comfort and security. If he held them close enough perhaps the pain would go away?

"Well, young man. You look as if you need some attention. Come with me."

She seized the handles of the wheelchair, turned her impressive bulk with astonishing speed and athleticism and led the way. Boadicea and her tribe meekly followed, in single file as the wheelchair, which no longer squeaked, streaked through the waiting room towards the treatment area. As if by magic the doors opened, swallowed up the entire group then silently closed behind them. Moses leading the Israelites through the Red Sea could not have done a better job. And then, just as the age of miracles seemed to be over, the door to the treatment room opened again and the triage nurse manifested himself, clutching a piece of paper upon which the name of one of the assembled company was inscribed. A moment of tension, a frisson of fear and hope; the wonderful terrifying second before lottery rollover numbers are drawn when everyone thinks it might just be them... then the name was announced. It was the woman with the sunglasses! She smiled apologetically and flung herself out of her chair. Thumb Man seized his chance and flung himself into it. The gammy leg buckled under the unexpected weight, cantilevered itself to one side and tipped him off the seat back onto the floor where it then joined him in one last feeble attempt to remain upright before it fell apart.

It was quite a diversion and went some way to alleviate the disappointment of all those left waiting. Tracy sighed heavily, mentally filling in the requisite accident report. Then there would be the health and safety review generated by the said report, followed by interminable triplicate paperwork and a departmental consultation with the legal team about Wyeminster NHS Trust policy regarding chairs collapsing in a public area. Then, as if that was not enough, a budgetary request would have to be made for a new chair, assuming that a chair was deemed appropriate and not some alternative form of seating more suited to the needs of whatever the Health and Safety investigation determined. It was depressing so, as she dug out an accident report form, she resolved to fill in only the most basic information and leave the rest for the next person who sat in her seat. Let the daytime lot deal with it. More of them anyway. Deciding to be distracted, she focused her attention on the nurse now talking to the woman behind the dark lenses. What on earth had he done to his face? Pulling herself forward with great difficulty so as to have a better view over the counter, she peered short-sightedly at his features, trying to work it out. He had been on his break she knew that much, but what in God's name had he been doing? Most people simply went to a quiet corner for a quick smoke, a coffee from the machine and a bite to eat but not Philip. Sorry, Francois. No, she had to get it right this time. What was it he wanted to be called now? Something transgender. That was it! Fronk.

The wand-shaped woman was following him like a hungry dog. Fronk was even thinner than she was, with startlingly short peroxide blonde hair and flesh tunnels in his ear lobes that you could put two fingers through. Of these he was immensely proud; it had taken months - years - of stretching them around ever-increasing discs to get them to their current size and shape. Outside work he liked to hang locked brass padlocks through the holes which made his head seem top heavy for his body and gave the impression of a blonde Weimaraner wearing a couple of overloaded suitcases. But lobe gauging was all part of Fronk's self-expression and no one much cared as long as he always wore the discs when he was at work. He had forgotten to put them in one day and the naked, flaccid loops of flesh, rosy pink and frilly, had been quite a shock. Not least to the patient over whom he was stretching when he caught one of them on the man's shirt button and could not escape. That was another occasion when the whole accident report rigmarole had had to be put into action but Fronk's flesh tunnels had stayed: an individual's right to self-expression in the work place out-ranked health and safety, even in a hospital. As long as he wore the discs.

By now however, Tracy had worked out what was different about his appearance. Eye liner! Thick, black and lustrous, his eyes had all but disappeared inside the barricades painted around them and it was difficult to ascertain whether his eyes were in fact open or closed, but as he seemed to know where he was going and was squinting meaningfully at the paper in his hand perhaps it was safe to assume that visibility was unimpaired and the effect was purely cosmetic. Clearly (hopefully) the patient he was guiding into the treatment area seemed to believe that he knew what he was doing so who was Tracy to comment? She returned glumly to the accident report form, all five pages of it, and reached for a pen.

Fronk was confused about many things but nursing procedure was not one of them. While he could never fully decide on his gender or sexual proclivities, he did know that a woman wearing dark glasses *a la* Victoria Beckham (whose clothes he adored – so sculptural) in an NHS Emergency Department might be in trouble

"I'm Fronk" he breezed as he led her through the treatment area to an empty cubicle. "May I call you Patricia?"

The lady looked embarrassed and uncertain. Avoiding his black rimmed eyes and gaping ear lobes she looked around the tiny cubicle for a chair, preferably with stable legs. She clutched her handbag and looked uncomfortable.

"Mrs Harvey. Thank you."

"Just sit on the bed, please, Mrs Harvey. Would you like to take off your sunglasses?"

No, not really, but she supposed she had no choice so, clutching her bag for support, she removed the protective lenses. Her eyes were blue, cared for, moisturised, or at least one of them was. The other was swollen shut and glowed purple black, fuchsia highlights, a touch of yellow at the edges. She could barely see out of it. Mrs Harvey avoided Fronk's scrutiny with her good eye and carefully folded up the sunglasses which she put in her handbag. Then stood. Motionless; exhibit A.

"Would you like to tell me?" Fronk meant what he said. It was a deliberately open-ended question strategy, designed by teams of psychologists and experts to elicit truth from patients who might also be victims. She had hoisted herself onto the edge of the bed and was perched there, still clinging onto her handbag like a handrail. Fronk had noticed her expensive hair cut – made Tracy's look like something with mange – and the way she had slipped off her shoes before getting up onto the bed. They were good shoes, polished, pristine-soled and very this season. Mrs Harvey was well brought up; no feet ever found their way onto on furniture in her life; footwear was kept clean; women were ladies and people did not use first names unless you were one of their own.

Mrs Harvey had gone to the loo, found blood in her urine and come straight to the Emergency department. It wasn't good, was it, to have blood in her urine? Should she be worried? It had never happened before. She sat on the high, hard narrow bed in the treatment room cubicle, dangling her pencil legs over the edge like a small child on a chair too big for them; vulnerable, frail. Not once had she mentioned her damaged face. It was as if it did not exist. Her aubergine framed eye dominated her pale face, Cyclops like, as she fixed a beseeching gaze on Fronk. No, it wasn't good he said, but he'd get the doctor on it as soon as. She wasn't to worry. But she would, and he knew she would and he also knew, as he drew the curtain across the entrance of the cubicle, that awkward questions would have to be asked. He would get Dr Mac to ask them this time – he could be very persuasive. It was going to be another long night.

As he was leaving, he turned to her and said, not for the first time,

"You know we are here to help you, Mrs Harvey. You just have to say." There was no answer.

Meanwhile, in another cubicle in the same area, Sister D was negotiating the Rosedales or, more accurately, the female of the species.

"My son must see a consultant."

"He needs to be assessed first." Delyth was adamant, but then so was Sebastian's mother. The male of the species, inferior specimens all, were silent. Sebastian because he could not speak, his father and brother because they dare not. "I'll get the registrar to take a look at him as soon as he's available and he'll decide if a consultant is necessary or not." Triumphantly dominant on her own turf, Delyth departed the cubicle without further speech or hesitation. She hauled the curtain shut with such vigour that the vulnerable disposable fabric was left swaying and shivering in distress while the hooks it hung on chattered with fear.

"I shall complain" Mrs Rosedale announced. "Leo. Make notes. Write down everything she says. Everything everybody says. Note the times, details, locations. Everything. We shall need it when we make a formal complaint."

The older man, he of the leonine nomenclature sighed silently and raised his eyes towards his good lady. If he was about to lodge an objection the moment was lost as she cut him off at the pass.

"Paper and pen in my bag. Mobile phone for photos. Felix. Hand them to him."

The other boy, the Rosedale's firstborn, named in honour of his lionlike father after whom he took in all things, especially his propensity to imagine himself depressed, mournfully began to rummage in his mother's capacious handbag. Eventually he found the required articles and handed them, ceremonially one by one to his dejected paternal role model. Hoping against hope, Leo tried the pen on the paper and found to his disappointment that it did indeed work. He carefully avoided his wife's eye but she did not notice – she never did. Her mind was invariably elsewhere.

"Felix. You take photos. Your father will be too busy writing. Everyone, everything. Start with Sebastian."

Chapter Two

Now that the ice had been broken out in the waiting room a convivial atmosphere prevailed. An animated discussion about peritonitis was in full sway, led mainly by Dawn and Shazza. Those two muses of all things medical were warming to their subject to the horrified delight of their audience. Having ascertained that peritonitis was indeed, poisoning of the blood – all of it, absolutely everywhere, so that the sufferer was riddled with it, keen interest was being shown in the exact nature of the ailment and all its manifestations. The description in hushed tones by Dawn of how the victim would swell up 'down there', coyly indicating her nether regions, before bursting, was met with appalled oohs and aahs of fascination, nurtured by her description of their unavoidable torment and agony. Nods of profound sorrow accompanied Shazza's comment that it was a terrible, terrible, way to go.

She spoke for them all; could not have put it better myself, can you imagine the pain? And the mess! Then they wanted details – how long would it take? How big did they swell? What burst first? Would they be able to see anything if it happened behind the closed door of the treatment room – blood maybe? Surely it would seep out into the waiting room? Or at least hear the boy explode? Surely it must smell, all that blood and guts? They would be bound to smell of something. When Dawn added almost as an afterthought that she had been reliably told by someone who knew because she had seen it, that everything went black and fell off, like gangrene, there was quite a party air and suddenly waiting for hours on end did not seem so bad after all. Not when there was something to look forward to. Tracy let them get on with it, reckoning that medical fantasy was less trouble than patient insurrection and she needed some peace.

Mac was struggling. Not mentally, he took things in his Australian stride, but physically. How did women do it? He had been carrying this baby for thirty minutes and was exhausted. Women carried them around for nine months and then the rest – new born, pre-toddler, toddler, right up to school age and then, more often than not, beyond. Carried. Not dropped. And then put down carefully; placed not dumped like weights in the gym. When he had offered to look after the young woman's baby while she went for a scan – yes, she did have to have one; absolutely necessary in cases of severe unexplained headaches – he had had no idea what he had let himself in for. At least the baby (he thought it was a girl but it was so difficult to tell) was quiet and well behaved. He shifted he/she/it onto his other arm and re-entered the noisy waiting room on his way back to the treatment area where he hoped against hope that nothing but one-handed procedures would be required, at least for a while.

Shazza spotted him first. Really, the evening was turning into quite an event and while an in depth-discussion of all things related to peritonitis was fascinating, the sight of a male medic clutching a baby while patently on duty was not to be passed over. Shazza nudged Dawn, which was easily done, allied as they were by natural affinity as well as close physical proximity: the distance between the chairs was not great and they required every inch of it to accommodate their hips.

"D'you think it's his?" Dawn hissed, just loud enough for everyone to hear.

"He's fit." Shazza replied, as if this was explanation enough. "Hunky." Then after a pause, "It doesn't look like him."

By now the waiting room had abandoned blood poisoning for genetics and a lively discussion ensued about who, how, when babies took after their parents. More inclusive a debate than peritonitis, everyone could contribute and indeed, everyone had an opinion to which they were keen to give voice. The increase in volume alerted Tracy who looked up from her accident form and swore.

"Frickin' hell, Mac. Where did that come from?"

Fortunately, the baby was too young to understand so could not be offended. Not so Shazza and Dawn who immediately took up joint umbrage on its behalf and glared at Tracy – ignorant cow – everyone knew where babies came from, and she worked in a hospital! No wonder the NHS was on its knees.

"Not mine, Trace. No worries! Only baby-sitting."

"You're not taking it in there?" She indicated the hallowed treatment room door.

But he had gone through it, baby in tow.

At first, Mrs Rosedale did not seem to notice the baby. She immediately accosted Mac as he carefully steered himself and his cargo through the curtain into Sebastian's cubicle, which was by now becoming rather crowded. Father and Felix were pressed up against the wall at the head of the bed like a pair of lions rampant on a heraldic crest, swearing allegiance to the recumbent Sebastian. None of them were moving; Sebastian could not and the other two were terrified of the wires, switches, buzzers and medical equipment attached to the wall behind them, against which they dared not lean. Naturally, Mrs Rosedale had the vanguard but both men knew to their cost that she also possessed an enviable ability of always being able to know exactly what they were doing, especially when you thought she was not looking. She would know if they transgressed and disobeyed her order 'not to touch'. Privately, Felix reckoned his mother had some supernatural extra sense. He would not put anything past her, especially not a member of the medical profession.

"Are you a consultant?"

"Not yet!" the babysitter answered cheerfully. "Dr Mackenzie. Registrar. And this must be… Sebastian" he surmised squinting at the notes in his free hand.

"You've got a baby!" Mrs Rosedale challenged, as if no one in the world should have children but herself.

"Not mine. Just borrowed while its Mum has a scan. Now Sebastian, what seems to be the matter?"

"I'm his mother" Mrs Rosedale announced. "He's got a burst appendix and needs immediate surgery. You must do something at once or he'll get peritonitis and die and it'll be negligence and we'll sue. He's only a child. Why are you looking after a baby?"

Mac completely ignored her; it was if she had not spoken and Sebastian had somehow thrown his voice in a masterly act of ventriloquism. Leo was appalled; Felix was in awe. The doctor seemed to regard Sebastian as the only person in the room and edged his way over to him, baby balanced in the crook of one arm while he gently pressed the boy's abdomen.

"We'll make a thorough examination first. Have you vomited?" It was hard to say if the boy wanted to answer or not, or to decide whether the anguish in his eyes was from acute discomfort or fear of his mother.

"Almost. Not quite. He felt sick in the car and wanted to, didn't you Sebastian?"

Sebastian looked at Mac and nodded, so slightly that it was almost imperceptible. He would have liked to speak for himself, but wasn't sure how.

"Sore throat? Runny nose?" Another tiny consensual nod.

"Bit of a cold, eh? Bet all your mates at school do too?" Sebastian agreed, silently but definitely. He even moved his head to one side to face the doctor; it was so nice to be spoken to directly.

Mrs Rosedale continued.

"It's not a cold he's got, it's acute appendicitis. He's presenting all the symptoms and is in terrible, terrible pain. I trained as a nurse so I know. And Google agrees with me."

The curtain moved aside and Delyth appeared as from nowhere, filling the aperture and metaphorically blocking out the light. It was as if the cubicle was cast into dark blue with white edges, the air became thinner and the temperature plummeted. Chilled and gasping for breath, Felix had a vision of Aladdin scrolling down a computer screen, whispering the magic word 'Google' and invoking some sort of malevolent, omnipotent genie that could turn them all to stone. Except his mother, who never noticed, never ran out of breath and never felt the cold. Far too busy.

"Would you like me to organise the tests, Doctor?" the genie offered. "You seem to have your hands full and we're very busy this evening." And it was settled, just like that. The doctor and the baby departed, Felix and his father were evicted as surplus to requirement and although Mrs Rosedale was permitted to remain, she was under instruction, "to keep out of the way. As a nurse you'll understand. Thank you."

Sebastian began to feel better.

Felix kept hold of his mother's mobile. He had always fancied the idea of photography and she was too preoccupied with Sebastian (as per usual) to miss her phone. She had refused to buy him one of his own – too young, too distracting and too expensive apparently – so she had only herself to blame and if his father noticed that he had slipped the mobile into his hoodie pocket, he said not a word. Nor would he. Anything for a quiet life.

The exiled Rosedales found the waiting room much as they had left it. Their return was greeted with interest but once it had been established that no part of Sebastian had turned black, gangrenous or burst, they were overlooked and retreated ignominiously to the far reaches of the room, away from Tracy, the treatment room door, hope and the toilet. In the pathological absence of chairs, they parked themselves on the floor, where Mr Rosedale assumed his usual stance of slumped despondency and Felix began taking selfies and artistic shots of his lower limbs.

Dawn and Shazza were discussing Mac. Shazza thought he looked like Russell Crowe in *Gladiator* and wondered what he would look like in a short tunic with leather straps and a breastplate. Dawn was struggling with the concept as she had confused her Russells. She could not imagine a skinny hairy comedian in any sort of tunic nor understand why he would want to wear armour. Shazza was in the midst of a long description of sweaty gladiatorial conflict as undertaken by Australian actors when, against the backdrop of the incessant phone with its three rings and everyone else's conversations, she was diverted by Dawn, who had had enough of Roman history and was absorbed in more recent events closer to home.

"Shh. I can't hear." Her attention was on a man, newly arrived, speaking at the reception desk. He did not know if Tracy could 'elp, but 'e'd banged his 'ead, a bit 'ard like, and wondered what 'e should do.

"No sign of any injury" Dawn confided to Shazza. "A bump like that, you'd expect to see something. Faking it. Hypochondriac. Typical chuffin man."

"I slipped on the kitchen floor. It was wet; and I banged me 'ead on the corner cupboard, the one where the wife keeps 'er cookery books. Not that she ever uses 'em. Anyway, she – the wife – said I should get it checked out. She goes on and on so I said I'd come down 'ere and get it looked at."

"Were you concussed?" Tracy embarked on the head injury protocol; standard admission procedure that she could recite in her sleep. Ha! Chance'd be a fine thing.

The man thought for a moment. No, not concussed, he said, not as far as he could tell. Did he look concussed? Tracy scrutinised his eyes over the counter, found nothing dilated, blood-shot, or of interest and shrugged.

"Hard to tell. Did it bleed?"

No, there had been no bleeding. Bit of a swelling there now but nothing else.

"Told you!" Dawn said. "Faking it!"

"Are you in any pain?" Tracy asked. No, not really. He had a slight 'eadache, that was all.

"Can you walk in a straight line?"

"Well I walked in 'ere alright."

"Blurred vision?"

No, he didn't think so. Could he see Tracy clearly? He peered suspiciously at her over the counter. There was a pause before he responded.

"I think so. … Is your 'air meant to be that colour?"

Tracy had heard enough but heads were heads, and had to be taken seriously, even if their owners did not deserve it.

"Sure it wasn't your wife that slung one on you for making personal remarks?" she joshed mirthlessly. "I'll put you on the system and someone'll assess you as soon as they can. Hospital policy for heads. Even yours. Name?"

"Andrez with a 'z' Lewinski spelled L E W I N S K I."

Take a seat Andrez with a 'z'. If you feel sick or faint, let me know."

"Can I sit anywhere?"

"Whatever takes your fancy. Preferably on a seat and not in a wheelchair."

"Over there?"

Tracy looked through Andrez with a 'z' and sighed, heavily, wearily, profoundly. But did not give up.

"Is there an empty chair?"

"No."

"Not there then. Somewhere else. Wait for an empty seat if you like; sit on the floor, hang from the strip light. Whatever."

Andrez was gazing around the room much as the captain of the Titanic might have looked at his crowded decks on being told that all the life boats were full.

"Will you tell me when I'm wanted?" he appealed to Tracy, as if begging for a life jacket. Someone would call him she threatened as the phone began to ring.

"What if I don't 'ear?"

The phone rang again.

"Then we'll get your ears tested. You'll know when they call you, trust me. I'll make sure of it." She picked up the phone and Andrez was dismissed, with or without his 'z'.

Fronk and Delyth – Sister D as she was known to the nursing staff – had a surprisingly cordial relationship. Both, in their way, were placed somewhere mid-gender and although Fronk might have been confused about his sexual identity, Delyth had no doubts about her own. She was self-partnered. By choice. It had nothing to do with sex or gender or anything like that but was founded simply on the fact that other people were intensely irritating and she could not be doing with them. Men, women, children – there was no discrimination. All as bad as each other and age seemed to have no bearing. Did people never learn? Senior consultants, adolescents, junior doctors, babies, admin staff – all of them and then the rest, most of whom seemed intent on getting in her way both at work and outside it. Delyth knew that if she could run the hospital as a dictatorship it would be a much happier, efficient and tidier place. She would not be unreasonable: enlightened maternalism would be the foundation of all her decisions but someone had to be in charge – no, that wasn't quite right. They had a chief executive who was ostensibly 'in charge' but no one was 'in control'. The Board of the NHS Trust were required (and deferred to, which appalled her) as a body to make important decisions so that was never going to happen anytime soon. What they needed was a leader, someone firm, informed, sensible and Churchillian. Someone like herself. The same went, of course, for the NHS and the government, but small beginnings. Delyth had plans and although she was approaching 50, had self-belief enough to thwart anything as insignificant as passing time. She should have been a doctor but her father would not allow it:

"Doctors are male. Men would be too embarrassed to see a lady doctor. You can be a nurse" he had decreed when she wanted to go to Med. School. When she had argued that women might not want to see a male doctor, she was told that that was different; women were used to being told what to do by men because they had husbands. It was a closed subject but had materially affected the way she felt about marriage. Authority had to be respected, she recognised that, even if it was misinformed. The way to get around it was to become the authority, and then you could do what you liked.

Fronk she tolerated. He looked like a freak but was professional, reliable and obedient, despite his anarchic appearance. All display and no substance she surmised when it came to insurrectional tendencies and rebellion. The conservatively dressed, superficially compliant medics were far more trouble. That was why she never took annual holiday in the summer, not that she took all her holiday entitlement anyway. Nowhere to go. Nothing to do. No, August was the month when junior doctors, those in their second year after qualifying, were released from captivity and let loose on Emergency departments throughout the land. Never get ill in August was all she could say about that.

She knew that everyone sniggered at her behind her back and called her *Carry On Matron*, but they were wrong. They might be a similar size and shape but Hattie Jacques' matron had a soft side, a weakness for senior consultants and a yearning to be loved. Delyth did not. Nor was she a snob; she despised everybody, without distinction. Her appointment at the Wyeminster was relatively recent and clearly designated. She had been brought in to troubleshoot, to turn things around in all things emergency. There had been some sort of recent scandal involving drugs and a staff nurse which had almost put the hospital into special measures. Well, it would not have happened on her watch and certainly would not now that she was *in situ*. The Hospital Trust had agreed to let her have almost absolute autonomy - within the confines of their hospital policies of course – and she had descended on their Emergency Department like one of the Four Horsemen of the Apocalypse.

Inheriting a department with resident staff was never easy but Delyth liked a challenge. She had a handle on most of the regular Saturday night crew. Tracy was gobby and truculent, but malleable. Occasional solicitous enquiries about her health, *gratis* paracetamol now and then, admire her horrible hair and she was on side. She might be sour but she managed a crowd. Mac – sloppy name but steady hands, even with a baby: depressingly chipper. His ebullience was exhausting but the patients liked him – made them feel comfortable they said. She would have liked to say that there weren't there for the comfort but recognised that calm clients were more co-operative so let it pass.

Fronk hove into view with Rohan. Rohan Patel. Trust Grade anaesthetist, working nights, always around but never when he was wanted. Something of the night about Rohan but she could not say quite what, not yet. Plump, not stately, with the texture and appearance of warm plasticine, more often than not damp with sweat, Delyth was waiting for Rohan to reveal himself. Not literally. Involuntarily she shuddered. Although no one had said anything she knew in her water that Rohan had been up to something, somewhere, sometime. Probably connected to the nefarious activity of the pre-Delyth departmental history. And she would find out. She always did. Meanwhile…

"Good evening, Rohan. Ah Fronk. Yes, good idea. Get Dr Mackenzie to see the suspected domestic violence. He's carrying someone else's baby … no, not like that … which might soften up our victim. Go with him as a witness. You're going in the wrong direction Rohan. Theatre is that way. Good evening."

Narrow-eyed she watched him toddle away from her down the corridor: flabby man on small feet, child-bearing hips in baggy blue scrubs, dark hair in need of a trim and a wash. Like Tracy's she had noticed.

Fronk found Mac at the far end of the treatment room already taking a precursory look at Mrs Harvey's file. The baby, which he had now identified as female, was sleeping surprisingly peacefully up against his chest despite being bent at an angle of almost 90 degrees with her head against the lumpy end of his stethoscope.

"Nice woman, saying nothing." Fronk said of Mrs Harvey while easing the baby away from the stethoscope. "Classy lady. Something to hide – apart from the black eye. Probably her husband is my guess."

"She hasn't said anything?"

"No. Acts like it isn't there but we all know it is. It's real shiner. She must've been really clobbered by something, or someone to end up looking like that. It looks like she's tried to cover it with make-up which hasn't worked, hence the dark glasses."

"What do we know about her?"

Fronk consulted his notes. "Not much. Married. Thirty-five. Lives in Cumberland Drive: well posh and pricey. All big detached houses behind gates with alarms and double garages. Well- heeled too – nice shoes. So clearly no shortage of cash, probably professional, definitely middle class. Anally retentive."

"She's presenting blood in her urine?" Fronk nodded. "You thinking what I'm thinking?" Mac asked.

Fronk nodded again. Repeated beating, thrashing, kicking or the like on the flanks could result in urinary tract infections at best, kidney damage or death at worst. Painful, extensive bruising was a given and just the evidence they might need, if she could be persuaded to tell them the truth.

"Mrs Harvey. Hello. I'm Dr Mackenzie, the registrar. I understand you have a UTI that we need to sort out for you?"

Mrs Harvey nodded. Mac registered her understanding of the abbreviation.

"Can we get a chair in here please, Fronk? I need to get the weight off my legs. How do you ladies do it, Mrs Harvey?" He indicated the sleeping baby which she acknowledged for the first time and half smiled. "Carrying them around for 9 months and that's just for starters!" She smiled a little more. "Do you have children?"

Yes, she did; a boy and a girl, at primary school. Well, the girl was, locally, but the boy had just started boarding at a prep school. She must miss him? Oh, she did. Dreadfully, but she knew it was for the best, so that he could get into the same school his father went to. They hoped he might win a scholarship; he was such a bright boy. She and her husband must be very proud of him. Oh, they were. Very. What did her husband do?

"He's a solicitor."

By now sitting on the chair that Fronk had found, who knows where, Mac was chatting amiably with Mrs Harvey who had begun gently stroking the baby's downy head and was softening with every touch. It reminded her of her own children when they were tiny; they grew up so fast. Where did the time go? So, when Mac asked her to put her feet up on the bed so that he could 'take a quick look at her' she barely noticed and did exactly as she was asked. Perhaps she could turn over on her side, that's it, just a little. He wanted to check her kidneys – standard procedure and then they would run some blood and urine tests. If she could just loosen her skirt at the waist a little. Lovely. Thank you.

Fortunately, her face was turned away from them, towards the curtain when Mac lifted up the back of her shirt so she did not see their reaction to the bruises on her lower back, extending down to her buttocks and beyond – they could not tell how far. Not without a full examination and that would take dark arts of persuasion to achieve. Her body was an abstract canvas of abuse. Fist sized, fresh, blue moons on her flanks from the blood in her urine; older strap marks on her buttocks and almost certainly the top of her thighs, yellow and green striations bordered by superficial abrasions like puppy teeth marks where the skin had been broken by what – a whip, a belt?

Mrs Harvey knew what they had seen, and that they knew. But she had not told them; had not uttered a word. Speak no evil. Not that He would ever believe her.

An uneasy silence filled the cubicle broken only by a faint snuffle from the oblivious child. Fronk and Mac exchanged looks; Fronk fiddled with one of the holes in his ears; Mac put his free hand onto the baby, as if to check that she was unhurt and whole. Then he softly replaced the shirt over the woman's back and hid her shame.

"We can help you, Mrs Harvey, you know."

She said nothing but readjusted her skirt and manoeuvred herself into a sitting position once more. She stared at her feet, then her lap, then the hands she placed there and the mass of white wedding gold and diamonds on her ring finger. The silence grew heavier, weighed on them, shut out the outer world and brought in the curtains even closer.

"I don't think so" she said.

"What about your children? Your daughter?"

"Oh, he wouldn't hurt them" she retaliated, looking up. "It's just me, and not all the time."

"Your husband?"

She realised what she had said.

"Everything you tell us is completely confidential, Mrs Harvey… Patricia. All we want to do is help. He need never know."

"He always knows. … Please. I don't want to cause trouble. I'm just here to get this infection sorted out; that's all."

More of the oppressive silence, tightening her throat, crushing her vocal chords. She would say nothing else. Mac had no choice but to move on.

"Fronk will take some blood then, and we'll need a urine sample from you. Then we can sort out medication but…" he hesitated, "we're always here. If you change your mind."

They both knew she would not.

"It'll have to be recorded" Mac told Fronk when they were out of earshot.

"What will?" Delyth the genie of the department had appeared, large and very blue.

"Mrs Harvey. Wife beating." Fronk supplied.

"Do you want me to have a word?"

"No" they both said together and startled the baby which cried out so all three leapt to the rescue and Mrs Harvey was on her own. Later she would leave, clutching medication for a urinary tract infection, just as she had arrived. Alone.

In the waiting room Dawn and Shazza had settled down for the long haul. Their friendship was now being firmly bonded over a shared love of illness, pain, personal misery, very detailed individual complaints and a mutual antipathy towards Tracy. Family illnesses, marital woes, inherited conditions and addictions would follow, lovingly embellished with detailed descriptions of all the calamities and agonies they had experienced, in person or by report, since the beginning of time. Well, they had all evening, hadn't they? Might as well make the best of it.

"Wotcha here for, Shazza?" Dawn had successfully opened the batting and her companion was running with it beautifully.

"Terrible sore throat. Agony. Can't swallow. Can't eat. Can't hardly speak. Nothing seems to help."

"Try keeping your mouth shut" Tracy muttered to herself.

"Tried gargling with TCP?" Dawn offered, the first in a Wiki length list of possible remedies. She knew them all – what hadn't she tried to ease her own suffering? Over the counter, off the shelf, doctors' prescriptions, herbal, homeopathic, healing crystals, hypnotherapy…oh she could tell you some tales. And all of them useless. Useless!

No, not TCP. Terrified she'd swallow some and poison herself, Shazza confessed. As if things weren't bad enough already. Honey and lemon didn't work either, or ginger, or any of the so-called lozenges that claimed to soothe and heal. Might as well suck an ordinary sweet or eat a vindaloo for all the good them throat pastilles did – and the price of them! At least a vindaloo spread the pain, as it were, so everything was agony from the runny nose to the, you know, 'other end' the morning after. Of course, she'd rung the doctor's surgery and tried to get an appointment but it was the usual story – no same day appointments and the silly cow on reception had said she didn't qualify as an emergency. As if she would know! Here, Shazza threw a look of disgust at Tracy as a representative of the lower order of medical receptionists who 'were no better than they should be.'

"So here I am" she said to Dawn. "No other choice. I don't mind the wait and they've got to see you eventually. It's antibiotics I need but try telling my doctor that. Right bloody minded she is about antibiotics; says they don't help. What does she know? She hasn't got my sore throat, has she? It's all very well saying it'll clear up of its own accord but she doesn't have to live with the pain, does she?" Dawn nodded sagely, understandingly, but ready to have her say now. Shazza did go on rather, especially when Dawn had much worse agonies of her own to discuss.

"It's my back" she confided, cutting Shazza off like a gangrenous limb. "I can't hardly move. Even sitting is torment. My doctor – a man, so what does he know? – told me to lose weight but how does that work when it's water retention? Barely a morsel passes my lips. Honestly. You'd be shocked if you saw how little I ate. But it's genetics, innit? In the family. We're all big. Born that way." Now Shazza was nodding in agreement, ready for a sprint start into her own point of view but Dawn beat her to the next sentence.

"I reckon I've slipped a disc the pain's that bad. Or my spine is broken. Crumbling into little pieces. Everything's connected to the back, isn't it, so I don't stand a chance, do I? If they don't cure me, I don't know what's going to happen."

Game, set and match. Shazza simply could not compete with such levels of a) suffering and b) gloomy long-term prognosis. However, she was a decent woman and could accept defeat with grace. She clucked sympathetically. The prejudice against big women was terrible, wasn't it? Ought to be laws against it.

"I'm starving. It's the stress" Dawn told Shazza as a finale to her lament. "It's all this waiting" she then shouted loud enough for Tracy to hear, but as Tracy had already heard every word of their conversation, she could have saved herself the effort.

"There's a machine in the corridor with crisps and things" Tracy broadcasted. "But you're not supposed to eat anything." Her flabby arm appeared from the depths of the reception desk and waved wildly in the direction of one of the many notices around the room requiring patients to kindly refrain from eating until they had had been seen by a doctor.

"No one takes any notice of those" Dawn confided to Shazza. "Not when you have to wait so long. We'd be dead of starvation before anyone got 'round to seeing us…. I could just do with a packet of crisps."

Shazza took the hint. "What flavour?" she said hoisting herself unevenly out of her chair which had braced itself under her weight and now bounced joyfully back into shape.

"Nothing with vinegar. Creates havoc with my stomach – terrible acid. It runs in the family. Probably an ulcer of course, not that I'm complaining. No point, is there? Plain if you have to … cheese and onion if they have them…" But Shazza had already gone, plodding determinedly between the rows of chairs and clients towards the corridor, wherever that was. She stood, grim, still and large when she encountered Thumb Man and the outcast Rosedales on the floor until they shifted aside to let her pass. Muttering ever more grimly to herself about the sorry decline in manners of the male population she not so much disappeared, as receded largely out of sight.

As soon as she had gone, Andrez with a 'z' made his move. Before Dawn could position a capacious buttock over the side of her seat onto Shazza's, she found it was occupied by he of the head injury.

"Oi! That's taken!" She was outraged.

"She's gone so it's not. 'Er loss. Anyway, my 'ead 'urts. I need to sit down."

"What's wrong with the floor?"

"Too low. Made me dizzy."

Dawn scoffed incredulously. "That's heights, not floors. She'll be back in a minute so you'll have to move. I'm keeping it for her…What's wrong with your head? Looks alright to me."

"Bit of an 'eadache…"

"Well you can't stay there so you'd better shift. Go on."

Resentfully Andrez heaved himself out of the seat, clutching onto the back of it for apparent support and unsteadily at first, moved away from the chair. All the rest were still occupied, as he ascertained from a vantage point at the end of the row by the magazine-free table, so he sighed loudly, ostentatiously rubbed his forehead as if soothing an embryonic third eye and shuffled untidily towards the exit.

"You haven't been seen yet" Dawn shouted at him as he made his way to the double doors which, ever alert, synchronised and professional, smartly stood aside to let him pass. Tracy at her station was immersed in her computer, the phone was ringing and an elderly lady with limited hearing was shouting her very personal details over the counter to the fascination of those nearby. Who'd have thought a woman of her age could have contracted something like that? You had to wonder how. Andrez disappeared without a word and the waters closed over him as if he and his 'z' had never been there.

Chapter Three

Mac glanced over the head of the sleeping baby down at his watch. How long did an MRI scan take, even at this time of night? Surely it would be quicker without the daytime queues? It wasn't that he minded holding the baby – she was cute, no trouble, soft and warm against his chest. He liked the way she had crumpled herself into the crook of his arm but her mum should be back soon, shouldn't she? What if the baby woke up and needed feeding? Or a nappy change? He had spent six months on Paediatrics: dealt with cardiac arrests in barely-there infants, premature-premature babies, sepsis, meningitis and God knows what else but had never actually fed a baby (except intravenously and that did not really count) or changed its nappy. The nurses did all that sort of thing, especially after the time when he had been examining a baby boy. Who knew that anything that size could pee so far, with such velocity? Fortunately, he had just finished speaking and his mouth was closed but he still suspected the nurses of some sort of bizarre initiation ceremony reserved exclusively for junior doctors. From then on, he had always simply covered the danger zone with an open nappy and swiftly moved out of range; let the nursing staff deal with it.

And where would he find such a thing as a disposable nappy in an emergency department at this time of night? He sneaked another furtive glance at his watch; wouldn't want baby to think he wanted rid. Perhaps something temporary could be done with packing dressing? But how could it be attached securely enough to prevent leakage? He'd give it another five minutes then call Imaging.

In the meantime, he was becoming quite adept at doing things one-handed. Good news if he ever broke an arm. Talking of which, they were just about to discharge a teenager who had parted company with a skateboard while attempting a double twist off a concrete ramp. The girl had tried to break her fall and succeeded only in snapping her ulna. She was now sporting a violent pink cast which glowed and illuminated the mottled red and purple of her upper arm, but was happy because her skateboard had been undamaged by the impact. Apparently, it was a top of the range specimen and they were inseparable. That was why she had brought it to the hospital with her and had it, even now, tucked under her good arm as she cheerfully marched away from the treatment room followed by her harassed parents laden like pack horses with their daughters' medication, clothes, elbow pads, knee pads, helmet, back pack, half-drunk can of coke, spare can of coke, collection of friendship bracelets from the now encased wrist and an emergency packet of crisps from the machine in the corridor.

Mrs Rosedale could be heard from behind her cubicle curtain berating the hapless Sebastian about the agony he had to be suffering while they waited 'for something to happen'. In reality, Sebastian was feeling more comfortable and less pained, and would have docilely drifted off into a peaceful slumber if only his mother would be quiet.

Mac took another look at his watch and had just begun fumbling in his pocket for his phone, mentally rehearsing the logistics of making a call one handed, when the missing mother appeared on the horizon like a vision, a mirage, some sort of preternaturally youthful fairy godmother arriving just in time to save the hero from an untimely death by soiled nappy. However,

Mac's cheerful greeting went unnoticed and he saw, with dismay, that she was white, trembling and tearful. Was it bad news? How could she know? Surely nothing had been said to her without recourse to him first?

She was a slight, winsome figure, as solitary in real life as she seemed in the treatment room. Desperation in the form of excruciating headaches had driven her into the arms of the Emergency Department early on a Saturday evening. Having no one at home to help out, no one to baby sit and nowhere else to go, she had brought herself and her baby by bus – as far as she could according to the weekend timetable - then on foot to the doors of the Wyeminster, where she wanted only 'something to take away the pain' so that she could return home and carry on. Fronk initially and then Mac, however, had both insisted that the headaches had to be investigated. It was a routine precaution; she owed it to herself and her child to have the scan; it wouldn't take long and they would find someone to look after the little one. At which point Fronk had been summoned elsewhere, Sister D was nowhere to be found, Tracy could not leave reception and the rest of the cupboard was bare. So, Mac said he would be delighted and honoured to help and had immediately detached the infant from its mother, who had been unceremoniously dispatched to the Imaging department and he had been left, holding the baby.

"Are you alright, Leila? Has something happened?" He was concerned. MRI scans were painless and routine; everything was explained to the patient and they were monitored and supervised at all times. Why was she so distressed?

"Come and sit down." He led her into the far cubicle on the corner, relatively private and reclusive. Maybe she was upset about the baby? "Look, she's absolutely fine. Never woke up and never even knew you were gone…"

Tears started to slip over her cheeks.

"Please tell me what's wrong." Mac was desperate. He held onto the baby, just in case. "Was it the scan?"

No, it wasn't the scan. That was fine. It was afterwards, when she was in the dressing room, getting changed back into her own clothes.

"A man came in and said it was a mistake but he didn't leave and then he … touched me."

The silence felt like a clamp, tightening around Mac's throat.

"A man?"

She nodded.

"What sort of man?" Damn. That's a stupid question he thought.

"From the hospital."

Shit. "Are you sure?"

Oh yes. "He was overweight with dark hair and was wearing blue. And he had those Croc shoe things on."

Would she recognise him if she saw him again?

"Absolutely."

The silence squeezed tighter. Mac considered what had to be done.

"Right" he said. "You stay here, Leila and look after the baby." He spoke almost as if it was his, or at least, theirs. "Would you like a cup of tea or something?" Coffee… He would organise that and be back as soon as he could. In the meantime, she wasn't to worry; she would be quite safe where she was – he would guarantee it.

Fronk was at the other end of the corridor.

"What's the matter?" he called as he sprinted towards Mac who was gesticulating wildly at him. "Where's the fire?"

Mac dragged him away, out of Leila's hearing, then pulled him conspiratorially close. Fronk didn't know he cared and was about to say so when he saw the look on the Registrar's face and all levity died.

"What is it?"

"The mother of the baby – she's been molested."

"What?"

"Here. In the hospital. In Imaging. While getting changed."

"Shit…. Who would do such a thing? Another patient?"

Mac looked past Fronk and around the room, the full length of it. Then he not so much spoke as inaudibly mouthed the words that followed, too terrible to be uttered aloud.
"It sounds like Rohan."

Tracy groaned.
"You're kidding? They'll crucify me." Nevertheless, it had to be done and the dreadful red words shone out from the digital noticeboard on the wall.
'Expected waiting time for non-emergencies 6 to 7 hours. We apologise for the delay."
"It's a bleeding disgrace, that's what it is." Dawn led the protest from her throne, Shazza at her side, everyone else in serried rows at her back.
"It's not my fault. Don't blame me!" Tracy retaliated but they did blame her, extremely loudly, because there was no one else. "If you're not an emergency, go and see your GP or consult a pharmacist" the script said. So, Tracy followed it and then wished she hadn't. Wished she wasn't there at all.
"At this time of night? Why the hell d'you think we're here?" Dawn spoke for them all, even though they were all speaking for themselves. "We wouldn't be here if we weren't urgent, would we?"
It was a difficult argument to counteract and Tracy wished, not for the first time, that she was a very great deal less visible. Another diet would start as soon as she got home.
"Why? What's happened? Why're we waiting so long?"
"I don't know and if I did, I wouldn't frickin' tell you lot" was the receptionist's considered retort but, in her defence, she did not know. Not really. All she knew was that all hell had broken loose somewhere beyond the treatment room, that thc Medical Director had been contacted and the police were on their way. The whispers said it was something to do with Rohan and Imaging but that was as much as she could surmise from the confines of her desk, to which she was chained without relief or respite. Sister D had borne down on her from her lair and told her about the delay – 'an incident' - was all she had said, mean

cow, and then expected her to deal with the fallout in the waiting room. What had Rohan possibly done in Imaging? He was said to be a letch, everyone knew that; couldn't keep his slippery hands to himself. Tracy had never known whether or not to believe the rumours and gossip but still, like any sane woman, never let him (or any of his kind) within an arm's reach of her person or allowed herself to be alone with him without recourse to at least one form of escape, physical or vocal. Legend had it that he was married with children but no one had ever met Mrs Patel or any of the little Patels, who, it was generally agreed, were much to be pitied. If they existed. But it was the perfect cover which had always made Tracy wonder. Children and a marriage certificate did not a happy homelife make. Tell her about it.

Podgy wattle-necked Rohan, blue scrubs, sweaty palms, sloppy Crocs, was always just there, wandering around the hospital, always on the way to theatre or just leaving it, without ever actually apparently spending any time in it. What could he possibly have done? And in Imaging? Where they were a funny lot, spending half their lives in little boxes and hidey holes watching TV screens while talking to contorted, motionless patients attached to machines. It was all that radiation probably; had to have an effect. The radiographers were the worst. Frustrated doctors and photographers or, in the worst cases, a combination of both. Their only pleasure the extent of the injury or a really complicated fracture that had them salivating over their PAC screens. Tracy had heard them talking in the canteen, getting all animated about someone else's bones while they huddled together in a gaggle and picked over their food. Not one of them was a vegetarian. Said it all really.

The noise in the waiting room was loud and increasing to the point that Tracy could no longer speculate uninterrupted. Fortunately, she was saved by the timely arrival of the boys in blue, or, to be more accurate, one boy and one girl (they did not look old enough to vote) not so much in blue as black. But their patrol car was parked outside and left its blue light flashing merrily along with those of the ambulances queueing outside. The effect was really quite festive and added a jaunty air to the occasion, quite in contrast to the instant silence that wrapped the room when they walked in through the double doors.

The police! It must be serious. All eyes tracked the heavy booted feet across the floor to Tracy, every ear was plucked and taut ready to listen, a string ensemble ready to play. Tracy even half stood up to mark the occasion and was about to speak when Sister D, fresh from her genie's bottle, revealed herself in the doorway behind and invited the officers to 'follow her'. They were admitted into that holy of holies, the staff entrance to the hallowed portals of Assessment and Treatment and vanished. Tracy resumed her semi-abandoned sitting stance, uncrossed her legs to avoid varicose veins and stared defiantly out across at the faces before her. They stared back, momentarily mollified, then the debacle began again. This time however, the insurrection assumed a different note. Clearly, Something Had Happened outside the usual complaints of staff shortages, incompetence, inefficiency, lack of resources, stroppy receptionists, all of which were shelved for another occasion while speculation and anticipation bred unchecked like salmonella on a warm day. Felix even stood up in his discreet corner and took photographs, which he promptly emailed to himself.

The unacceptable waiting time was now, magically swallowed, whole. There was even a general review within the room about what constituted a serious injury. Thumb Man ruefully examined his maimed digit and decided that as it was not bleeding and appeared to have attached itself more securely to the rest of his hand, that maybe it could wait until another day. He shifted uneasily on the floor, then made the momentous decision not to stand, walk and leave. Nothing to go home for. Not so many of the other men and women but not those with children in tow, who all elected to stay. There was a steady exodus of shamefaced not-as-urgent-as-they-thought-they-were-after-all patients shuffling to the exit and the double doors were quite exhausted by the unexpected one-way activity. To a person, the departing wounded avoided Tracy's gaze so only those remaining witnessed the triumph on her face. However, victory was not entirely hers. Dawn, with Shazza following closely behind, resolved to stay and 'sit it out'. In fact, nothing was going to move them. Saturday night, an Incident, law enforcement, front row seats and now packets of crisps for sustenance. What was not to like? Dawn would have preferred cheese and onion flavour to plain but, well, you couldn't have everything.

Behind the scenes of the public forum, Emergency was in a ferment. Mac had told Sister D. what had happened and been astonished by the ferocious efficiency of the woman. He had been immediately dispatched to contact the Medical Director who had instructed him to call the police. Leila and the baby (still asleep) had been moved to an office with a comfortable chair and supplied with coffee, biscuits and a Friend of the Hospital who had just happened to be nearby, according to Sister D. Mac suspected that both the office and the Friend had either been conjured up out of nowhere or kept in a cupboard somewhere 'just in case' – he would put nothing past the redoubtable woman. It had made sense to remove mother and child from the curiosity of the likes of Mrs Rosedale, who was now quiet and listening intently to every whisper and nuance. Neither Felix nor her husband would have believed she could be so attentive to anything that did not pertain to Sebastian or herself. At least the exiled Rosedales now had seats out in the waiting room. Indeed, so many not-so-urgent-after-all had left the premises that quite a few of the chairs were vacant and it was possible to select a vantage point from which to watch proceedings. And it wasn't even closing time! Goodness, it was exciting. So much to look forward to. Dawn and Shazza could barely contain themselves but, to the immense relief of all those around them, managed to curtail their enthusiasm and gave it large vocally rather than physically.

Chapter Four

Tracy knew Graham Parsons, the Medical Director by sight but had never had a conversation with him. When the tall, thin slightly stooped figure shambled through the double doors - that treated him exactly like everyone else - she was surprised when he approached the reception desk but managed to find the kind of scripted smile and cheery greeting of which her line manager would be proud. He looked more like an aged bookseller or a time-serving back bench MP than a doctor. Always wore the same dark suit of vintage proportions, slightly shiny on the buttocks from too much sitting on unforgiving NHS chairs, a magnolia shirt with frayed cuffs, brown brogues and a red knitted tie. Topping off the ensemble was a pale face under a receding hairline with a pair of half-moon spectacles over which he would peer so much that people wondered why he wore them at all. He spoke softly, without an accent – the only clue to his public-school education about which he never spoke, nor the listed Georgian manor in which he had been brought up. Neither sat easily with his determined Methodist faith and his political beliefs, which he kept to himself.

He was a rheumatologist, which he always said with a sigh, knowing that he would have to explain what that was. No one ever knew. You never saw dashing rheumatologists saving lives or performing miracles in hospital dramas on the television. Nor indeed was he the dashing type in any sense of the word. Everything about him was ascetic and measured – movement, speech, thoughts, actions. Even his smile which emerged gently, stretched carefully over his own, perfect orthodontically engineered teeth then receded at exactly the same pace as it had arrived. He did not drink, did not eat refined sugar, avoided anaesthetists and played the violin with a passion that sometimes frightened him.

The waiting room assumed he was just some old buffer with a medical problem and was checking in.

"Poor sod" Dawn whispered to Shazza. "He's got no idea how long he'll have to wait."

When he immediately disappeared out of sight into hallowed ground however, they were more intrigued than outraged.

"Doesn't look like someone in authority." Dawn sniffed derisively. "But you can never tell these days, can you?" And of course, Shazza agreed.

It was Sister D who had sat down with Leila with Mac as a witness to find out exactly what had happened and she it was who took the MD under her wing to bring him up to speed. Mac was remitted to continue practising medicine while the call had been put out for Mr Kirmani, the on-call ED consultant. He was in the building, that much they knew. What they did not know was that he was already on the case, having been alerted by an alarmed colleague in Imaging and was even now in the process of extracting Rohan from theatre, like a rogue appendix, for investigation and examination.

Sister D. began the briefing. Graham Parsons might be the Medical Director but he was only a man.

"She was in the changing cubicle getting dressed after her scan. The door wasn't locked – she was in a hurry to get back to the baby so didn't bother. Didn't think it was necessary at this time of night."

Doctor Parsons nodded. She had a point.

"A man came in, apologised for the mistake but didn't leave."

Sister D paused. Get to the point the MD looked at her.

"He went closer to her – those cubicles are very small – and stroked her arm…. She was wearing an NHS gown and was naked on her top half underneath. Apparently, he touched her breast."

"Through the gown?"

"Yes. It wasn't fastened. Well, they never do, do they?"

Dr Parsons nodded sagely, visualising the flimsy, over washed, over worn cotton garment that had the audacity to call itself a gown.

"Then what happened?" He had to ask.

"The girl was frightened but didn't scream or say anything. Too shocked, I think. She said the man suddenly stopped and left. Just like that, without a word. There one minute, gone the next."

"Is she a sensible girl?" Not a question he should be asking, he knew, but it was said in such a measured way that somehow it seemed acceptable. And everything depended on the answer.

"Very."

"Are we sure it was Rohan Patel?"

"Almost certainly. She described him exactly and says she can identify him … Will never forget him."

"Hmm. Anaesthetist, isn't he?"

"Trust Grade."

Another thoughtful 'hmm'. Not as expensive as a consultant at least, but suspension on full pay pending an investigation would be unavoidable. Required.

"Police?" he asked.

"With Leila now. She's a single mother, young baby, capable, nice girl. … Reliable witness." Sister D spoke like a telegram (she abhorred text language).

"Let's get on with it then" he said, peering over his half-moon lenses with his eyebrows chasing his retreating hairline.

Leila liked Dr Parsons and felt confident telling him exactly what she had told Sister D. whom she had found less sympathetic and who blocked out the light. It was also precisely what she had told the police, who were still in the room, one cooing over the baby, who ignored it all and continued to sleep.

"I only came in for a headache" the harassed mother wailed. "What happens now?"

It was a good question and the answer lay with her. Did she want to bring charges against the accused? Yes, they did know who he was and no, she would not have to meet him in order to identify him. She hesitated.

"Will he be arrested?"

Only if she made a formal complaint. He would be charged with indecent assault, arrested and taken into custody according to police procedure.

She was horrified. Not surprisingly, her headache was much worse and Sister D disappeared to organise pain relief.

"I don't want to cause any trouble" she wailed again and to everyone's surprise, including his own, Dr Parsons found that he was quite distressed on her behalf.

"You're not, my, er, dear. None of this is your fault and I'm sorry that it has happened. Whatever you decide, he won't stay in the hospital and you are perfectly safe. You have my word."

It was not like him to make such rash promises but it seemed to work and she stopped wailing, although the baby chose that moment to wake up and begin, as if taking up outraged reins on behalf of her mother and setting off at a gallop to make up for lost time. By which time Sister D had returned with life-saving paracetamol and Leila had decided she just wanted to get home. A police statement would be necessary but that could be done at the station and then they would give her a ride to her house if she wanted? She did, and the male police officer was thrilled; he was still holding the howling baby who was beginning to quieten under his auspices which made him wonder if he had chosen the wrong profession.

The problem of further distressing Leila by a formal identification of Rohan resolved itself by the astonishing cooperation of the perpetrator himself. He arrived at the MD's office on the second floor virtually at the same time as the MD and they switched the lights on together, as it were. Rohan made no attempt to deny that it was he who had gone into the cubicle but insisted that it was a genuine mistake; the door was unlocked, he had no idea that anyone was in there, he was looking for something, but did not say what. She was wearing an NHS gown, yes, but seemed to be struggling with the ties so he tried to help her but she seemed to have got the wrong idea and when he realised that she was not happy, had left. Immediately. He'd done nothing wrong, not intentionally anyway; it was all a misunderstanding. Very unfortunate and he was very sorry but it was just a mistake and she had got the wrong end of the stick. No harm done. Thus ended the defence.

Mr Kirmani who had escorted the accused and witnessed this oration, was as flummoxed as his boss, the MD. The female police officer, who had no interest in babies but deeply resented any infringement of women's rights and personal space fought hard to maintain an appearance of impartiality and repressed the urge to slap him. If only she could cuff him to a radiator or something. She looked forward to the moment she could legitimately arrest him and woman-handle him into custody, still in his baggy scrubs and Crocs, but for that pleasure, she would have to wait.

On television it was always all about reading the accused their rights and summoning legal-eagle representation but in the setting of a stark NHS strip-lit Medical Director' office in a regional hospital on a Saturday evening, the atmosphere was more sad than breathless. Although it was the first time Graham Parsons had had to suspend someone with immediate effect, he knew the procedure. It was the sort of thing you learned, by rote, when put in post, but hoped never to use. However, he had already contacted one of the Trust's legal department 'just to be sure'. Measured was good, but absolutely by the book was better.

"You will be immediately suspended, Dr Patel, on full pay, while the Trust conducts a full internal inquiry. The burden of proof for that investigation is the balance of probabilities – 51% - rather than beyond reasonable doubt, 99%, as required in criminal cases. Of course, if the young lady chooses to bring charges against you, that is her prerogative and a matter for the criminal courts."

He chose to ignore the sudden arrow-eyed gleam of satisfaction on the face of the female police officer and continued.

"As the Medical Director I will appoint an impartial case investigator and I will personally act as the Case Manager to ensure that everything is conducted in a fair and proper manner. You will be escorted from the premises", here he had no option but to acknowledge the obliging police officer who was already reaching for her handcuffs, "but before you do so, have you anything to say?"

Rohan had slumped further into his scrubs and seemed to have shrunk in height but sadly not in width. He looked wrung out, like a badly washed duvet, all lumpy and saggy and uneven. Everything about him was moist, from his greasy hair through his damp hands to incipient tears making his eyes bulge and spill. It should have been impossible not to feel sorry for him. Certainly, opinion was divided in the waiting room as he was led through to the exit. He looked pathetic – harmless enough. If only they knew what he had done.

Tracy had a pretty good idea. It was something about the way Rohan walked – unresisting yet defiant, head held up and back straight but eyes covert, sly, hooded. Unseeing. Unrepentant. It was never his fault, just like it had never been her mother's. They had been led on, tempted and provoked. Only giving the bitches what they deserved, then being punished for it. They were victims, not criminals. Tracy saw not Rohan being led out of the waiting room but a prematurely aged young woman with cold eyes and a soft voice. The pink nylon quilted dressing gown she usually wore had been replaced by tight jeans and a pink nylon top, braless, which had been hastily donned when the police had arrived. Eventually. She had not even looked at the daughter who had called them. After that, Tracy preferred to look at her only in photographs and ignored her stepfather completely. She kept to her room, propped a chair under the handle, ate alone and always wore long sleeved tops because she hated her arms. The camera did lie, no matter what people said. Big fat lies. Smiling faces did not make happy families.

As it had been deemed sensible to keep Leila and her now once more quiet baby in the comfort of the secluded office until the coast was clear – and her medication could be sorted out and obtained from the pharmacy, which always took forever – the connection between them was not made by the amateur sleuths in the waiting room. By the time Leila left, unnoticed, to be taken off to the police station long after Rohan had already arrived, the general consensus about his crime was one of manslaughter by neglect at best, murder by lethal injection or something intravenous at worst (or best, if you shared Dawn's view). Felix got some very lucrative shots of the departing fugitive with his police escort - artistic and expressive - which was exactly what the editor of the local newspaper said when the story broke.

En route to his department, Mr Kirmani bumped into Mac. The Medical Director stayed in his office to begin the paperwork, muttering inaudibly about anaesthetists and resenting his loss of the cheeseboard at the church safari supper he had been forced to abandon. Did cheese count as a vice? If it did, then he would go to his fate well-nourished and without regret. Mac heroically resisted the temptation to ask about Rohan and instead, regaled with Mr Kirmani with the saga of The Rosedales.

"She's convinced that her precious Sebastian's at death's door with a burst appendix."

"And is he?"

"Not even close. I suspect she thinks I don't understand the English medical system – because I'm Australian. Apparently, the symptoms of acute appendicitis are different in the Antipodes and I clearly don't know what I'm doing."

Mr Kirmani raised one hairy eyebrow. This might be a welcome diversion from the gall of an alleged sexual assault. Mac gave him the details as they walked towards the scene of Sebastian's suffering, then stood back as the consultant prepared to engage.

"Are you a consultant?" Boadicea challenged as soon as he pulled the curtain aside.

Mrs Rosedale knew he was not – he looked far too untidy and where was his suit jacket? But it was a line of questioning that seemed to work and gave her an immediate advantage from a position of righteous superiority, hence had become her opening gambit of choice.

"I am."

Before she could react, the expert pressed home a substantial lead.

"Mr Kirmani. Emergency Department Consultant. Mrs Rosedale, I understand?" He offered his hand as he looked through her. "And this must be Sebastian…"

It was, but a key line of defence was not to give the enemy time to speak so Mr Kirmani glided on blithely, judiciously oblivious to anything that the devoted mother might want to contribute.

"Mrs Rosedale". He gazed directly into her eyes and fired. "Your son absolutely does not have appendicitis. I can assure you that his appendix is not about to burst and he is in no danger of developing peritonitis. Google tends not to be as reliable a source of information as an on-call registrar who's examined the patient. Although he is presenting some of the symptoms associated with appendicitis, Sebastian has a condition called mesenteric adenitis - inflamed lymph nodes in his abdomen caused by a virus. Painful but not serious and certainly not life threatening."

Magnanimous in victory, he took pity on her.

"So, there's no need to worry. We'll run some more tests and keep him in overnight for observation but there is no cause for alarm."

Now it was the vanquished mother's turn to be magnanimous and her performance did her credit. Her gratitude was boundless – heartfelt. Mr Kirmani – his department – the hospital - were wonderful. She had been so frightened, terrified that her darling boy was dreadfully ill; that she was going to lose him. How could she ever thank him? She was sorry if she had been a little abrupt with his colleague, the Australian. Or was he from New Zealand? It was so hard to tell; they all sounded the same, didn't they?

Mr Kirmani's hairy eyebrow rose again, involuntarily, and he was tempted to ask where she thought he was from: India,

Pakistan or some other dark corner of a once glorious British Empire? But he was a professional and opted for a parting jibe before he moved on to more pressing cases.

"My dear lady. It's natural; you are his mother. Now it might take a while to arrange a bed for him; we're very busy tonight – but I'm sure you won't mind waiting, will you? Someone with your medical background and experience."

And he was gone. Mrs Rosedale did not feel as elated as she would have expected. She had the vague idea that she had somehow been reduced in size but could not for the life of her, work out how.

Fronk meanwhile was trying to cope with the ever-increasing influx of patients arriving through the indefatigable double doors. At least he could assess them, if they chose, once they had seen the writing on the wall.

"Andrez Lewinski" came the voice from the doorway.

No reply.

"Andrez Lewinski?"

"With a 'z'" Tracy added.

Fronk stuck a couple of fingers through one of his ear lobes, as if he expected to find a missing person on the other side. The more recent patients looked at each other enquiringly… You? … No, not me…. Nor me…Shame … and sighs of disappointment ensued.

Mr Lewinski? Anywhere?" Third time lucky. Maybe he was in the toilet, or doing battle with the coffee machine in the corridor?

"Came in about 30 minutes ago? Mid 30s, dark hair, jeans? Banged his head on the kitchen cupboard after slipping on the wet floor? Wife sent him for a check-up?" Dawn the ever helpful had spoken and even Tracy could not help being a little impressed – that was exactly what was written on his admission details. She wondered for a brief second if Dawn had breached the Data Protection Act, (ooh, she'd have her for that) and taken a sneaky glance at her computer screen, but then reassessed the size of the woman and knew it was a physical impossibility. Maybe she had second sight? No, just acute hearing.

"He was that loud. Couldn't help listening" Dawn explained "Could we, Shazza? Bet he wasn't the one washed the floor. Not a man I know of would think to wash a floor." She returned to her public.

"He's gone. Looked fine to me but not very happy. Probably the waiting…He tried to take your chair, Shazza, but I put him right on that."

Dawn and Shazza began a mutual condemnation of the male species in kitchens, waiting rooms, lack of manners, inability to do housework and prepared to thoroughly enjoy themselves.

"Did you see him go, Trace?" Fronk asked.

"Nope. News to me. His choice. He was worried about not hearing his name when it was called but I didn't realise that'd be because he'd left the building."

Fronk was not surprised; it happened all the time. One less patient for him to assess and process so no loss. Just as he was in mid-turn, about to begin the next check-out item on the conveyer belt of pain, the doors opened and a disability scooter hove gently into view. It bore a leviathan of a man in green tweed, with matching cap atop a face of cardinal colour and proportions. He was deftly guiding his vehicle towards Tracy with one hand and holding a Big Mac in the other, from which he took monstrous bites which pouched out his cheeks like a hamster preparing for hibernation. A sticky trail of mayonnaise and ketchup tinged with mustard sauce was to be seen flowing serenely down his unshaved chin, colourfully coating the stubble to add texture then on, down his neck (what could be seen of it) onto the pasture of his tweed belly, where it came to rest, exhausted; unable to surmount the huge hill of flesh in its path to venture any further. Here it joined ranks with dried egg, a selection of assorted crumbs of dubious heritage and a coffee stain.

The man parked himself carefully on the other side of Tracy and called to her over the reception desk counter.

"Got a pain in me belly."

"I'm not frickin' surprised".

Not quite the response specified in her receptionist's script but an interpretation that highly entertained the waiting room. Dawn and Shazza abandoned the subject of male ineptitude and turned their attention to the disability scooter.

"Now that's what I need." Dawn pronounced, green-eyed. "Just the thing to save my back and legs. How fast d'you think it goes?" She cast lascivious eyes over its neat buttock-wheels and six pack parcel storage space, its muscle-bound seat and broad handlebars. "Even room for sticks and a handbag" she said approvingly, liking very much what she was seeing. Meanwhile its occupant was inelegantly detaching himself onehanded from his carriage with a great deal of heavy breathing, gasping, stopping, starting, biting, chewing and slobbering over the burger in his other hand. Only as he had finally deposited himself on *terra firma* did he finish his repast. He wiped his mouth and chin with sticky fingers which he then smeared on his capacious chest which was beginning to resemble an edible work of art by Jackson Pollock.

Once he was standing it was possible to see his exact proportions and to marvel. Such size, so much tweed. Dawn felt quite svelte by comparison and Tracy was dwarfed … but not deterred.

"You want to see a doctor?"

"Yeah. Sore belly."

The waiting room examined the abdomen in question and was not surprised. So much flesh. Where would he sit? How would the doctor find anything? Was an assessment even possible?

Tracy bowed to the inevitable and began to enter his details onto the system.

"Take a seat." she said without looking at him. "You can't sit on that" she said hardly pausing for breath as he made to turn back to his winged chariot. "It'll have to stay here." So, with great effort, the elderly Billy Bunter heaved his way over to the nearest available chair which braced itself and gritted its teeth in preparation for the burden that was about to descend. The chairs on either side commiserated and shifted aside; their chum would need all the space it could get.

Chapter Five

Fronk was smugly satisfied with the steady pace of the conveyer belt – a sort of rhythmic chain gang, striking steady and consistently along the cubicle highway. He was an efficient gang master; assessment was the starting point for everything else in the system. He had stamina and form; the prolonged wait for treatment after assessment was not his problem and as long as he maintained a constant flow of patients in and out of his domain then all was well. However, even he was disconcerted by the size of the green tweed gent and feared for the safety of the bed in the cubicle. Indeed, for the cubicle itself. It took some time for the patient, and his abdomen, to puff and blow his way to the receptacle which unfortunately was at the far end of the room and Fronk felt unreasonably resentful at the dent this made in his time and motion data. He checked his Fitbit and pursed his lips, then did an impromptu on the spot jog to up the total. The invalid was complaining of a stomach ache and Fronk was not looking forward to the examination.

"Where does it hurt? Start big and work in.

"In me belly". Fronk surveyed the contours before him.

"Whereabouts?"

The invalid, whose name really was Billy although his surname was not Bunter, pointed a chubby digit at an egg stain on his chest, slightly below what could have been a substantial right nipple – it was hard to tell. Probably his liver, Fronk guessed, and ploughed on.

"When does it hurt?"

"After eating. Not straight away though, 'bout half an hour. Comes in waves."

"Every time you eat?"

"Yep. Bleedin' agony it is. Enough to put me right off me grub."

But not quite enough, by the look of things, Fronk kept to himself as he breezily announced that height and weight would have to be measured, BMI worked out and Billy's diet assessed.

"I'm not on a diet." Billy protested. "Never felt the need."

"What I meant by diet is what you eat, day to day. Do you eat a lot of fried food for example?" Fronk was examining the vestiges of the man's dining experiences encrusted on his tweedy chest like a badly positioned row of medals and insignia in the process of sliding down over his stomach on their way to a more southerly campaign.

"No more than the next man. I like me full English of a morning but I don't have chips, not every day, or stuff like that."

"What about burgers and takeaways?"

"That's not fried, that's burgers. Meat, veg and bread. Nowt wrong with that. Good basic food and plain tastes, that's me. Can't be doing with all this fancy foreign nonsense. Only takeaways I have are English. Fish and chips, pie and peas, saveloys. Tried a Chinese once and was hungry ten minutes later."

As he spoke Fronk could almost see Billy's liver – enlarged, pale and discoloured, pitted like sandstone exposed to the pitiless elements for too long.

"Do you drink, Billy?"

"Not much. Just enough to be sociable."

'Just enough' again, registered Fronk and made a note on his assessment sheet about the possibility of the effects of excess alcohol on the tormented organ. He also wrote gallstones in capital letters with an enormous question mark that hung over it like gallows.

"Right then Billy, we'll get you weighed. Can you walk to the machine? No. Okay. We'll have to bring it to you then. Just wait here and someone will be back in a minute or two. Any problems, just press that red button there" ... He pointed to the alarm on the wall behind the bed. Better to be on the safe side – never knew when a heart attack could strike although it rather looked as if Billy would have some sort of seizure if he so much tried to twist around to reach the button.

On his way out he commandeered one of the health care assistants to perform the height and weight exercise on Billy.

"My bet's a BMI of at least 50. If it's lower, I owe you a coffee. Bloods as well – diabetes, liver markers, cholesterol…good luck with finding a vein."

Tracy was struggling. Everything was aching, her head was pounding, she was tired and she was sure her ankles were twice their normal size. Had she forgotten to take her anti-depressants? No, she would never do that. Maybe she needed to up the dose? She shifted from buttock to buttock on her unforgiving chair and tried to raise up her legs in an attempt to drain the swelling. This was awkward and uncomfortable and meant that she could not easily reach the computer or the phone. Never mind; she would take what respite she could when she had the opportunity and there was a can of Red Bull in her bag. No sooner had she perched herself in this recovery position when the double doors opened – again – did they never stop? – and a young woman appeared. Slowly. She was supported by an older version of herself; both wore the same tight jeans, skin-sucking low-cut tops over rigid breasts with deep, dark canyon cleavages. Outsized hoop earrings bounced on their shoulders under bleached hair pinned up in top knots as tight as their clothes. Mum, who was the elder by about twenty years, had an artistically manicured hand under the elbow of her daughter whose trout pout was contorted with pain. She could barely walk. It could not be blamed on her shoes. While Mutton dressed as Lamb expertly manoeuvred on vertiginous wedges, Lamb wore feathery pom-pom mules, low heeled that slide-clopped their agonised way across the hard floor. Tracy was intrigued, first by the sound, which transported her back to childhood, then by the footwear itself. She abandoned comfort and strained to see better. My God! She shivered. The last time she had seen shoes like that they had been slippers, worn by her mother, beneath the pink nylon dressing gown. Her mum had looked like a soft Dalek wearing its hair in heated rollers, with a cigarette instead of a ray gun. And now here they were, at the bottom of a pair of jeans, slap-clopping their way across the floor towards her desk. Coming for her. She heard the hearty clack of the solid heels on the floor and started to sweat. She felt the fear; tensed herself for the impact and tried not to react. When the blow did not come it was somehow worse; it meant waiting for the time when it would. The welts would appear later, big bruises that spread like rainbows across her flesh but she would be the only one to see them. She stroked her fore arms, clenched her thighs and swallowed the bile in her throat.

"It's her butt" Mutton said, with no attempt at discretion. The sourness in Tracy's mouth made her gag but she forced herself back to the present. No one seemed to have noticed. The waiting room had immediately concentrated their attention on the bottom in question and everyone was listening except Mr Rosedale, who dozed upright on his chair. His espoused was still with Sebastian who was now on his way to a ward, but she had omitted to update the other members of the pride with the news so they continued to wait. They were used to it. Felix focused the phone on the woman's very pert, substantial posterior and hoped no one would notice.

"What's wrong with it?" Tracy asked, *sotto voce.* Her throat was tight; memories hurt.

"What? Speak up love." Mutton spoke even more loudly, as if to compensate for Tracy's soft tones. So Tracy spoke up, to the joy of the seated audience straining to hear.

"She's had a butt lift that's gone wrong." Mutton explained. "One side's dropped. Absolute bleeding agony."

All eyes beamed in on Lamb's buttocks, consciously weighing them up. Thumb Man lifted his injured digit into the air and squinted past it to the object of interest, like a painter measuring the human form.

"Looks alright to me" Shazza muttered but Dawn was not listening. She had taken the opportunity of the diversion to make a move: slow, heavy, but motion nevertheless. Shazza assumed she was repositioning herself to get a better view. Dawn was on her feet, standing, testing the floor with one foot after another and making as if to walk; an elephant, new born, tentative, finding its feet and balance in an unfamiliar world.

Tracy peered over the counter with almost as much effort as Dawn's elevation and studied the butt cheeks in question.

"Which one?"

Mutton turned her offspring around so that Tracy could get a better view.

"The right, but it's hard to tell – the jeans are holding it in."

"They're tight enough" Shazza hissed, in vain to Dawn, who was staggering laboriously in the direction of the toilet.

"Can she sit?" Tracy asked Mutton, as if Lamb did not exist.

"No!" the latter screeched, proving that she did.

"Better get her assessed then" Tracy announced wearily, back on task, preparing to contact Fronk. He'd like this one, she thought – makes a nice change from the usual Saturday night fare. She'd never booked in a butt lift before and wondered what she should call it. Did it count as an emergency? Kim Kardashian had a lot to answer for.

Dawn had ambled as innocuously as possible across the room towards the toilet but had not stopped there but merely paused, as if taking a breather, before heading with grim determination over to the unsuspecting disability scooter, parked at one – unseen - side of Tracy's reception desk. Unseen by the receptionist that is; Dawn had been eyeing it ever since its owner had vanished with Fronk into the sanctity of an assessment. She wanted a closer look; it was winking at her with its shiny metal handlebars and capacious black leatherette seat. How comfortable it looked! Not too big, not too small, but just right: exactly like

Goldilocks and the three bears except that this was a hospital waiting room and she was somewhat older than the fabled golden-haired heroine. No less adventurous though, so while all eyes were focused on the lopsided butt of the most recent addition to their number, Dawn decided to act. With a speed and agility astounding in one of her proportions, she suddenly found herself ensconced in the seat, feet off the floor and hands gripping the controls which, although sticky with what appeared to be coagulated mayonnaise, thrilled. The power! The speed! The open road! Thus, she moved, first from one story to another (was this how Toad had felt?) then into reality, as she turned the ignition key which Billy had left in its snug little compartment ready for a swift getaway (and because he had been unable to see it over his vast stomach). The scooter, always anxious to please, leapt into immediate action, surged forward and made a beeline for Mutton whose earrings bounced in alarm as if to sound a warning.

Mutton leapt out of the way; Lamb could not. Although Dawn steered the scooter wildly to the left in an attempt to prevent a collision, it was too late and Lamb went down as Dawn went off - at an angle, straight into the wall below the digital noticeboard that shuddered, hiccupped, danced a jig but held. It was the only thing that did. Dawn trembled as an earthquake aftershock, the scooter buckled and died from the front in the kind of death reserved for black and white B Westerns. But the real casualty was Lamb who lay, prostrate, on her back, where she had fallen, screaming.

"It's burst! I can feel it!"

At last! Something had finally exploded. While they were, of course, pleased that Sebastian's appendix had not erupted there was also a secret disappointment but patience is a virtue and rewards come to those that wait, at least that's what Shazza told Dawn afterwards when she described the event in minute detail for the benefit of her friend still perched on the scooter. Dawn could hear more than see – so frustrating – but Shazza made up for it later and Dawn was still able to tell everyone that she had been there, yes, at the precise moment that it happened.

The screaming was primeval; real pain; sustained and relentless. Medical personnel appeared from every direction; health care assistants and cleaners; porters normally never to be found; nurses, doctors, Mac, Mr Kirmani, Sister D and Fronk. (But no anaesthetists). Treatment and Assessment was a desert, the waiting room the hub of the world and all while the screaming continued, not even pausing for breath. A trolley appeared; Lamb was lifted, turned and laid upon it then wheeled off at a speed that could only make the disability scooter's damaged eyes water. The procession disappeared leaving only the crash site and the walking wounded to the mercy of the spectators and Tracy.

Dawn was helped down from the seat of destruction and deposited, considerably less gently than Lamb had been, onto the nearest chair which buckled under the sudden weight, but held, to Tracy's relief. Another broken seat was the last she needed in the light of the form filling this latest episode would require. Health and Safety would go berserk. There was the damage to the wall, the noticeboard looked wonky but was still working although some of the message now appeared to be labouring uphill as it looped its endless way across the screen and then there was the issue of the scooter itself, which was Not Her Problem, thank God, but someone would have to pay. She eyed Dawn and sucked in her teeth. "Now you've done it" her expression said and the moisture on Dawn's upper lip defied gravity and travelled north to her eyes, which began to spill and leak.

In his cubicle Billy had no idea what had happened. He had heard the commotion and the fleet footed exodus of those around him but they soon returned and he was relieved to hear Mac tell him that rather than being about to die, he was suspected of having gallstones – nasty and painful but easily sorted. He would need to come back for an ultrasound scan on Monday morning and then possible surgery to remove them.

"Surgery?" Billy was shocked.

Mac understood; the prospect of surgery was daunting, perhaps terrifying. He switched into super-understanding I share your pain mode and began to explain the procedure with well-practised, calm reassurance.

Billy was having none of it.

"Not eating before? For how long? I can't not eat. I'll starve."

When Mac told him that the nil by mouth time would be at least eight hours, there was a horrified silence.

"I can eat before this scan thing though, can't I?" Not so much a question as a challenge. Mac braced himself.

"I'm afraid not. Nothing to eat for at least six hours beforehand. … Plenty of time afterwards though to make up for it!"

Billy simply glared at him, whether in disbelief or in the early stages of post-traumatic stress disorder it was difficult to say, but was saved by hearing that, in the absence of any inflammation markers in his blood tests, he could go home. Once he had established that this Dr Mac, as he called himself, whatever kind of name that was, would not be involved in the procedure on Monday he felt a very great deal better and the pain in his abdomen seemed to subside. All he wanted to do now was get out of this madhouse, resume his place on his trusty steed and get the hell out home for a nice cup of tea and a restorative snack. His blood sugar was low; it'd be a wonder if he didn't faint. If he started eating as soon as he got home and paced himself, he could make up for the time he would lose starving before scans and surgery. His mind turned to the wonders of the twenty-four-seven supermarket on the outskirts of town; thank God he had transport.

Lamb really was about to faint. She lay face down on her trolley and howled, especially when she was half rolled, put on a board thing and lifted by many hands onto the bed in the cubicle, still face down. She buried her foundation, lipstick, mascara and blusher into the paucity of the thin paper sheet rolled out on the bed as the howls became moans. Removing her jeans was a problem and, in the end, it was decided to incise rather than peel. Mutton objected – they were 'well expensive designer' but Lamb did not care; they could have been Giorgio Armani himself and she would still have said "Cut". Mr Kirmani did the honours, hovering with his scissors over the right butt cheek for a moment as any good surgeon would, reverentially selecting the spot and girding his loins for the sombre act he was about to undertake.

He would start with the waistband and work down, caring hands following and anticipating the path of the blades in order to gently pull aside the denim as he progressed south. It was a solemn performance, increasingly quiet as the pain relief jabbed into Lamb's arm worked its magic.

It was like skinning an overripe tomato but eventually, the deed was done and Lamb's booty was revealed for all to see. And marvel. One butt cheek was pale, solid and smooth. The other was red and angry – incandescent – and they could almost see it throbbing. Both were protuberant: two minor planets, one cool and dry the considerably larger other a tight, swollen, stretched carmine beacon of pain. When touched it seemed to roar and Lamb, now revealed as Chardonnay squealed with renewed anguished when it was touched, even ever so gently. Her current pain relief could only dull the agony, not block it completely and the strength of her language bore testament to its inadequacy. Although the prosthesis was not actually exposed, it had clearly decided to make its presence felt and had slipped down her butt towards her thigh, as if it was trying to make a getaway down her leg. The jeans had, indeed, been acting as a restraint and once removed, the prosthesis bounced into life and shivered energetically, ready for the off, an overweight greyhound in the slips.

"It'll have to come out" Mr Kirmani said, unnecessarily. Even Chardonnay's mum could see that.

"She'll have to go into theatre under a general anaesthetic so that we can open up the wound, remove the stitches and the implant, drain the pus and clean everything up …we don't want her getting sepsis – a very serious infection….

"What about the other one?"

"I'm sorry?" the consultant was confused.

"The other cheek – the good one." Mutton was fighting an uphill battle. What was wrong with these people?

"Oh, that's fine. Nothing wrong with it. There's no need for us to touch that at all." Mr Kirmani thought she would be relieved.

"You're not going to remove it?"

"No, there's absolutely no need."

"But she'll be lop-sided! One butt'll be bigger than the other. How's she supposed to walk? And sit down? She can't have half a butt! Her clothes won't fit."

Mr Kirmani could see her point and sympathised, he really did, but it was out of the question that they would undertake any kind of surgical cosmetic procedure on a perfectly health bottom cheek, especially as an emergency. They would treat the infected cheek, of course, as soon as they could get the patient into theatre which had to be soon to avoid further problems. But as for the other one – well, her GP would have to refer her and then she would go on a waiting list for treatment and, no, he could not say how long that would take but the waiting lists were rather long. Perhaps they could go back to the surgeon who had performed the original implant? …

"Where did you get his done?" he asked.

"Turkey" Mutton replied.

"Turkey?"

"Yeah. We got a deal. Two-week holiday with one procedure included, boobs or butt. Me and Chardonnay had our boobs done last year. They did a great job – look." She proudly put her shoulders back and thrust her chest forward for the consultant to examine. He leant back, she followed and offered to let him have a feel.

"They're not hard or anything. You'd never know the difference. They gave me a larger size than I asked for but it didn't cost me extra. Chardonnay's are just as good, aren't they love? Not as big though. We've never had no trouble with them so we thought the butts'd be the same. Mine are fine." Upon which she swung round and twerked for the benefit of the attending medics who retreated, as one, into the immovable safety of Sister D who stood firm behind. Mr Kirmani led an untidy withdrawal of forces through the curtain and out into open space, leaving only the heroic Sister D to prepare the patient for theatre and to dispense with – in any way she could – the mother. At least the latter seemed now to be coming to terms with the shock of her daughter's disproportionate posterior.

Outside the cubicle, some way down the corridor at the oasis of the water cooler, Mr Kirmani and Fronk stopped running and took stock.

"Christ!" the consultant said to the man with the holes in his ears.

They were assailed by the high-volume commotion from the waiting room by way of answer, which did not in any way relieve Mr Kirmani's anxiety. Billy had emerged from unforgettable horrors in Assessment and Treatment only to shuffle morosely into the security of the waiting area and the prospect of freedom to find that his scooter, his precious wheels and passport to mobility, was impaled in a wall. The front wheels were buckled, the handlebars twisted, the paintwork scratched and scoured; it was festooned with flakes of NHS paint and plaster from the wall against which it was slumped. The trusty basket at the front, that fount of so many comestibles and his friend in times of hunger and need was nothing but a flattened tangle of bent wires. Beside the scooter, sitting on a chair, was one of those two women he had seen earlier – the gobby one with the crisps. She looked as dishevelled as the scooter but decidedly less damaged as she gazed up at him and he Knew. It. Was. Her.

Now Billy was not violent, nor prone to ill temper (unless he was hungry) but there is only so much a man can take, especially with the prospect of medical procedures on the horizon, and Billy had reached that point. He felt it as a physical pain (or maybe that was the gallstones but no matter). He lunged at Dawn, who recoiled, but could not move fast enough to defy the gravitational power accelerating the descent of the giant frame of the man onto her person. There was a horrible spongy sort of thud as they collided and then a tremulous clatter as they both hit the ground alongside the scooter which shivered, shifted, lost its balance, gave up the will to live and fell on top of them. All Tracy could think about was the paperwork resulting from the destruction of another chair. Hell, at this rate there would be none left by the end of the night and the Trust would be holding an effing forum on the subject.

"I'll sue!" Billy was scream-breathing as he was helped upright by a battalion of concerned onlookers, wounds permitting. Dawn was not, however, going to go quietly.

"You shouldn't have left the key in! It started itself! It's not my fault – my hands slipped. You shouldn't have sticky handlebars. It's your fault!"

"It's a write off!! How'll I get around? How'm I going to get home and go shopping?... I've got gallstones." The tragedy of Billy's condition was only now beginning to sink home. He seemed more vulnerable than huge and waiting room sympathy was all his. Dawn was definitely to blame; should mind her own business; it was a hit and run; that's what happens when you nick cars and joy ride; lucky no one had been killed; where were those police officers who were here earlier? Never a policeman when you needed one – it was an absolute scandal the lack of police on the streets these days.

Mr Kirmani simply wanted them gone. Sister D was summoned from the bedside of Chardonnay to take charge, to disentangle and restore order. Billy was collapsed into an extra sturdy size wheelchair and as swiftly as one porter could manage, hastened to the double doors which could not wait to get rid of him. As a victim of a road traffic accident, as Billy was now calling it, he wanted to call the police, report Dawn for theft, have her arrested, handcuffed or ankle shackled (the Yanks had the right idea) taken before a magistrate so that he could sue her for damage to his property, consult a lawyer and have the personal telephone number of the Trust Chief Executive so that he could make a full complaint in person. He would also contact the Press, local radio, Citizen's Advice and that man who runs Facebook. So, a taxi had been arranged but had to be replaced by a minivan to accommodate his bulk along with the corpse of his scooter. Once both were safely off the premises, *en route* to the supermarket and then home, Dawn was left to face the discord – and Tracy. Who was ferocious. The forms to fill, the reports to write, the changes that would be made: intense high-level Trust discussions would follow regarding future arrangements and regulations for the parking of disability scooters, designated parking bays would have to be provided, checklists compiled for the removing of keys, insurance details, proof of ownership. Oh God, it did not bear thinking about, so she glowered at the guilty party now occupying her original (unbroken) chair and confined herself to murder by sight. She and Mr Kirmani both.

"She can't go. she hasn't been treated" Sister D informed the consultant when he saw Dawn.

"Anyway, she needs to tell us what happened for the incident report and then the inevitable health and safety report."

"It's nothing to do with us!" Mr Kirmani's hairy eyebrows were thorny and had moved close enough together over his nose to shake hands.

"No, but it happened on Trust premises" Sister D explained, patiently and slowly, as if talking to the hard of hearing. Honestly, consultants were such a trial. Children in all but their own field of expertise and sometimes even then, they needed guidance. She thought of the Professor of Haematology she had once worked with: always had his head in a research paper so walked into everything and everyone in his path. Which was fine as long as he was the one who was injured but hard on the patients and staff. One of the porters ran a book on him – how long would it be before his next collision? The record was three minutes which, although impressive in terms of timing, was less lucrative than had been hoped as there had been insufficient time for people to place their bets. At least Kirmani wasn't one of those, but it was always best to keep consultants out of public areas if at all possible. They just got in the way.

Chapter Six

She was wrong. After the event it seemed as if some sort of divine intervention had decreed that the ED consultant was standing, albeit perplexed, in the middle of the waiting room. They heard the sirens approaching, getting louder, bluer, more insistent, calling, calling. Then a pause before the doors heaved apart, flinging themselves wide to make room for the trolley, the feet, the people, the equipment and the tension. Leading the procession was a man in green, massive chested, more biceps than body, squeezed into his uniform which struggled across his chest in exhausted creases while it attempted to make up for lost space by escaping from the waistband of his trousers.

"Resus! Suspected brain haemorrhage. Male, mid 30s. Unconscious. Nice to see you Sister. Coming through!"

Tracy joined in, anything to relieve her fury,

"Everyone! Out of the way!"

There was a cacophony of scraping chairs, shuffling feet, the noise of possessions and the paraphernalia of extended waiting being shovelled across the floor or lifted into the air as the entourage made its entrance and shot across the stage towards the treatment area. Sister D and Mr Kirmani joined the procession, a macabre conga of ever-increasing length and speed. Dudley, the paramedic was issuing orders as they followed:

"Right pupil dilated; GCS 6; needs intubation and ventilation. Coming through."

Sister D looked like a thunder storm trying to hold its breath; Mr Kirmani's eyebrows were winged caterpillars, circling his forehead with astonishment. But as Dudley would inform him later, he was a professional, a paramedic, not an ambulance driver, with over twenty years' experience and that was on top of his military service. It was an assessment like his that made all the difference between life and death, on or off hospital premises. He was confident that Mr Kirmani would agree; pulled himself up to the top of his five foot ten inches, tucked his shirt into his waistband as if reaching for a small firearm and luxuriated in his superior wisdom when the consultant did not argue. Not that there was any point, because Dudley was always right, even when he was wrong.

"That'll screw the waiting time" Shazza muttered gloomily as she attempted to comfort Dawn in her hour of need.

But there was more to come. Barely able to draw breath after their momentous parting, the doors were at it again. This time for a woman, alone, running, dripping wet and smelling of fear she landed herself in front of Tracy.

"The man. That just came in. He's my husband. What do I do?"

"Stay calm and tell me his name."

"It must be raining" Shazza decided, studying the newcomer's wet clothes and hair.

"Andrez Lewinski" the woman said.

There was a silence. Everything stopped, time stood still, suspended in the moment. Even the digital noticeboard climbing its way up itself on its eternal loop halted, and seemed to listen.

"With a 'z'?"

They all strained to hear.

"Yes."

Tracy's headache was forgotten as she contemplated Hell.

"He was here earlier this evening but nobody would see him so he came home again. He banged his head and he seemed alright, but then he wasn't." Mrs Lewinski, more puzzled than tearful, was only saying what most of those listening already knew. Tracy tried to claw her way back.

"He left before he could be assessed. What happened?"

Now Mrs Lewinski began to cry.

"He slipped on the kitchen floor. I'd just washed it and he skidded because he wasn't wearing shoes, only socks."

"Told you it was a woman who washed the floor" Dawn told Shazza. "Marvellous how a diversion can take your mind off your own aches and pains isn't it?" she added, philosophically. The scooter accident was already becoming just a ghastly memory, although it would resume its glory and terror when she recounted the adventure to sympathetic audiences.

"Yes, yes." Tracy knew all about the slipping on the floor bit. "But after he got home, Mrs Lewinski, what happened then?"

"He said he felt dizzy and sick and then he sort of had a fit and collapsed. That's when I called the ambulance."

Mac materialised from the unseen beyond.

"Mrs Lewinski?"

"Yes" she and Tracy said together.

"I'm Dr Mackenzie, the Registrar." He extended a hand in greeting which she never even noticed, so intently was she watching his face.

"Could you come with me please, and tell me exactly what happened to your husband?"

Dawn and Shazza would have been more than happy to explain and save that poor woman the trouble – the distress - but no one had bothered to ask, so they stayed where they were and imagined the unseen conversation, providing very convincing emotional outbursts and oratory to the admiration of those around them. Their performance however, was wildly understated and woefully underplayed the real drama taking place behind closed doors. Had they but known! When Mrs Lewinski saw her husband and was shocked, not so much by the equipment and people around him but by his appearance; he did not look like her husband. His face had changed; he wasn't Andrez. He looked far away, removed: empty. Although his eyes were open, they were unseeing, blind. He appeared to have sunk into his own features, crumpled. It was if the ventilator breathing for him was pumping him up against a slow puncture; as fast as it inflated, he lost air and deflated like a flabby balloon.

"We believe your husband has severe bleeding on the brain" Mr Kirmani said. "It's very serious."

"Is he going to die?"

The suddenness of such a direct question was in some ways a relief. It meant that they did not have to pussyfoot around the issue and that Mrs Lewinski understood the exact meaning of 'very serious', that they would not have use euphemisms to explain the unexplainable and that she was most probably the kind of person who would cope with the worst outcome. It did not however, make their immediate task any easier. But they could at least, be honest.

"Not if we can help it, but he needs urgent treatment. We're taking him for a CT scan which will give us a clearer idea exactly what's happening. We're concerned about increasing blood on his brain so we may have to perform an emergency operation to relieve the pressure."

"Operate? How?"

"It's called a Burr Hole procedure. We drill two small holes into the skull and drain off the fluid. Then the neurosurgical team will be able to get to work on him in theatre to try and repair the damage…Will someone get Mrs Lewinski a chair please? Now."

Tracy was being tested. He said his name was Colin – didn't give a surname – and that he had an emergency. Except it wasn't him exactly, but the patient was terribly ill and he was afraid he was going to die. It was to do with the way he said "Colin" when she asked him for his details, that made Tracy's hopes shrivel, as if he was the only one and she must know him. He said he worked in Davinia's shop in the High Street, well, it was Davinia's but she had been promoted and now they were getting a new manager. Or manageress. He hoped it was a manageress. He liked for working for a lady manageress. Tracy was about to point out that most manageresses were in fact, ladies, but the man was talking with such uninterruptable determination that diversion was impossible. A consultant had worked in the shop, he said, and was such a nice man. He'd told Colin all about The Hospital and The Emergency Care and how marvellous it was and it was for everyone so if he had a problem that's where he should go for help. So that's what he had done and here he was and he really hoped they could help because he'd found him floating upside down and not moving. Well, he thought it was a him, but it was always so difficult to tell when they were in the water.

Was it? Tracy had absolutely no idea what he was talking about. Apparently, they never stayed still and the water distorted your view and you could not see undernea…

"Slow down, Colin….Oi. Colin!" She had to shout to make him stop, which he did, mid-syllable, slightly shocked. He did not like it when people shouted at him. It was rude. Mother said so.

"Are you saying there's been a drowning? Have you called an ambulance?"

"Should I have done?"

"For an incident in water? Yes! When did this happen?"

Every soul in the waiting room tingled with excitement, rapt with attention. A drowning! In Wyeminster!

"About tea time. I'd just made myself a cheese sandwich and sat down to watch television and then I saw it."

"Tea time!" Tracy gasped. The waiting room gasped, *en masse.* The double doors wondered if they should open for an infusion of fresh air and oxygen, a sort of an industrial scale resuscitation.

"But it's…" Tracy looked at the digital clock … "after 10.30! Where is he now? You haven't just left him?"

Colin was scandalized. Of course not! What did they think he was? No, he'd brought him with him. They'd taken a taxi. It was an emergency wasn't it? Besides, it was raining and there were no buses at this time of night, especially not on a Saturday. He knew, he used the buses a lot but did not like to travel before 9.30 in the morning because then you couldn't use your bus pass and you had to pay.

By now Tracy and the entire waiting room were in a state of nuclear meltdown.

"You brought him in a taxi?"

"I held him very still, so he didn't get jolted."

"How's the rain going to make any difference if he's drowned?" Dawn asked Shazza, speaking for the whole room.

"Where is he now?" Tracy asked. Bewilderment did not even begin to cover it and she feared for the answer but the question had to be asked. She wondered whether mental health would be available at this time of night – there must be someone to do some sort of emergency assessment, but whether for herself or Colin was not clear.

"Here."

Colin held up a supermarket biodegradable plastic carrier bag, creased with careful clutching, a little damp and dripping. There was a bulge in the bottom which trembled slightly as he lifted the bag, the top of which was neatly tied several times,

"to prevent leakage".

"In there?" Tracy started to look for the number of the emergency mental health unit. "He's in there?"

"Yes…Do you want to see? Or should I wait for the doctor?"

Tracy was nothing if not valiant.

"I think I'd better take a look" she said, reluctantly, and began to shift her buttocks into the 'off chair' position. She leaned over the counter to peer into the bag which Colin was carefully untying, gently and lovingly.

"I don't want to frighten him" he explained.

Everyone there sat up, perched upright, squinted - anything for a better view. All eyes were on Tracy, their vicarious vision, as she leaned over a little further and her face began to disappear into the receptacle.

Everyone waited. Nothing moved. The doors were paralysed with fear, the very air stopped breathing, the digital noticeboard faltered and froze. An eternal second, transitory, endless yet non-existent.

"It's a fu …ish!" she proclaimed to the world, much as the Christmas archangel bringing the good news to those waiting on the hillside. Only Colin was not surprised.

"What did you think it was?" he asked, perplexed. "D'you think there's any hope? When can he see a doctor?"

The babble in the waiting room was such that Colin barely heard Tracy tell him that he could not see a doctor not now, not later, not ever if she had anything to do with it. What did he think this was? A frickin' zoo?

"But the man outside said you could help."

"What man?"

"The one washing his hair. With no clothes on."

Tracy stared, genuinely perplexed.

"He was very polite."

"Washing his hair?"

"Yes. It's pouring now."

Tracy stared some more. Colin explained. Really, this lady was quite rude; it was rude to stare. Mother said so.

"With rain. So, he can rinse it. … His hair."

Still fixed on Colin's face, Tracy contemplated the alarm buzzer below the desk but was saved by the arrival of Fronk, on a mission of triage but distracted by the haunted look in his colleague's eyes.

"Everything ok, Trace?"

Colin looked relieved.

"Are you the doctor?" He held up his carrier bag expectantly.

With the kindness of one used to dealing with the criminally insane, Fronk shook his head, took Colin's arm and wheeled him towards the exit where the doors parted in telepathic understanding and swallowed up the man, the bag, the fish and what remained of Tracy's sense of humour. Outside the man had finished shampooing his hair and was standing, arms akimbo like the Angel of the North, enjoying the sensation of the bubbles running down his naked body as the rain hammered onto his soapy head.

By now, Dudley, discharged from the responsibility of organising the ED team over his recent delivery appeared, or rather, loomed over the proceedings and assumed control. Not that he was ever not in control, of course, but it was always a case of perception. Thor-like he raised his arm and his voice; the nude man heard, lowered his arms, dashed to his clothes, hat, toiletries and joint sheltering under an empty Big Mac carton and scuttled away like a foamy Gollum.

Colin followed, dripping and wet, clutching his carrier bag and wondering where he would find transport at this time of night. But he need not have worried; it would soon be closing time and there would be taxis aplenty. Then all he would have to be concerned about was the disposal of his deceased companion.

Mrs Lewinski had been returned to the waiting room. They would have liked to put her somewhere more private but there was neither time nor space so she found herself seated between two fat ladies who began to cluck over her. They had made space for her the moment she had materialised in the doorway so naturally she had gravitated to the vacant chair, winking at her with the promise of soft bellied maternal comfort. The one who called herself Shazza began.

"There, there dear. It's your husband that's the emergency isn't it?"

She nodded tearfully. "Yes. A brain haemorrhage. They've got to drill his head open."

Dawn oohed sympathetically as her eyes boggled.

"Must be very serious?" Shazza continued. "Are they doing it now?" Dawn strained to hear the reply as well as any indication from behind the scenes of incipient drilling. What should she be listening for? A Black and Decker type electric drill or perhaps something higher pitched, sharper, along the lines of a dentist's?

"They've got to burn a hole or something and then they drill into his head to empty out the blood. He might die."

"No!" Shazza was thrilled. "And all he did was slip on the kitchen floor?"

Mrs Lewinski was crying. "I'd just washed it…I shouted at him when he fell for not wearing shoes. And now he might die."

"Shoes would've made the floor dirty though," Dawn suggested. Mrs Lewinski began to howl.

"D'you think we'll be able to hear the drilling?" Shazza asked Dawn behind the back of the weeping one. "It must be quite loud."

"Not if she carries on like this – we won't hear a thing."

"Ssshh don't cry." Shazza put a cellulite dimpled arm around the afflicted wife and offered consolation. "Don't worry. If he dies you can sue."

"What?" The crying stopped abruptly. Dawn took up the cause.

"Yes. That's right. He came in here earlier this evening. We saw him, didn't we Shazza? No one treated him and then they sent him home and now he might die. That's negligence, that is. Plain and simple." Then after a pause she added, "I blame the receptionist."

All three turned their gaze towards the reception desk and the top of Tracy's head visible above the computer screen.

"Tracy, they call her." Shazza said. "He never even saw a nurse."

Other than the even breathing of the ventilator and the hum of monitors, it was quiet. Mr Lewinski lay serenely in front of his standing audience which was focused, for the moment, not on him but on Mr Kirmani. Even the on-call anaesthetist was looking at the consultant. The neurosurgeons had not yet arrived; something had to be done to relieve the pressure on Andrez's brain or there would be no need for them.

"His wife's well out of the way?"

"Yes".

Mr Kirmani nodded to Mac, brandishing a pair of electric clippers like an antiseptic sheep shearer.

"Shave the head please, Mac … where I've marked."

Mac started the clippers which gently buzzed their way through floppy hair. He kept within the lines, neat and careful, his best colouring in. A perfectly circular bald patch appeared on the man's taut-skinned skull, slightly shiny, stretched and pink. Mac turned off the clippers, the buzzing stopped and he stood back not to admire the neatness of his handiwork but to allow Dr Kirmani to inspect it. Pronounced okay, all eyes then swivelled to the image on the screen above them where Andrez's brain scan was projected: huge, larger than life but hanging onto it by a gasp.

"We don't want to drill in the wrong place."

It was better to say it than not; everyone was thinking it and yes, they were all in it together although the consultant knew that this was his call, his responsibility, and if it went wrong, he would have to answer. This was what being a consultant came down to … the salary, the private practice, kudos, sharp suits and well-fed ego actually counted for nothing at times like this. No one now wanted to be standing in his leather-soled shoes.

They surveyed the head swathed in sterile sheets before them, the hairless patch of skin cleaned and prepped, slightly pockmarked like a plucked oven ready chicken. Mr Kirmani made a small three-sided incision into the skin to produce a flap, a window, a trap door into which he would make the hole. Lifting the skin, he studied the fat and muscle below for a moment before raising them too, revealing bone: Andrez's skull.

"Ready?"

There was a short blast of high-pitched drilling. Very short. Sharp. The sound drowned out everything else and seemed endless but in fact lasted only seconds. When it stopped it felt as if the ventilator was breathing for all of them. As the singing of the drill died away, all eyes turned again to the screen, just to check. No one spoke. Mr Kirmani, steady handed, immobile, scrutinised the image on the screen and prepared to continue.

They all resumed their focus on the sterile skewer on its entrance into the skull and the drilling resumed. In the waiting room, Shazza and Tracy were sitting, ears stretched, imagination rampant, Mrs Lewinski between them like a fledgling in a nest. They heard nothing.

Another burst of drilling. Anxious eyes turned to the screen to check, and check again.

"A couple more and we can put in the drain. I'm looking for a spurt of dark blood under pressure" the consultant told Mac, without moving his eyes from the swathed head. "Then I know we're in the right place."

The soprano trilling resumed, reached a short crescendo and stopped. Died away. To be replaced by the monotone of the monitor, flatlining.

"Hell."

"He's arresting."

"CPR! Adrenaline. Defibrillator on charge!" Mr Kirmani's voice – louder than the others. No panic but bustle, frantic, fast, each second critical and vital while time was ebbing away. The carefully counted rhythmic thumps of Mac, hand over fist, pumping the chest of the impassive Andrez; the ventilator breathing but the body not; the rising electronic whine of the defibrillator as it girded its electrical loins. And always the monotone of the monitor, flat lining.

"Stand by to shock." Everyone stood back as instructed but not needing to be told.

There was a bang. Andrez's chest lifted with the impact, then dropped. Inert.

"Again."

Another fleshy bang, the chest leapt up, more in earnest this time. But then it dropped down and lay, quiet, supine, motionless. Apart from the relentless unbroken song of the monitor, there was silence.

"CPR Mac. Keep it going."

Mac was sweating with the exertion. He concentrated on counting, pressing, pushing and praying. Twenty minutes passed. Then twenty-five.

"Hell" someone said again.

Someone, he never knew who, gently touched Mac's arm.

"Do you think he's had enough?"

Everything stopped.

"We've lost him" Mac hardly believed his own words. He shook his head and wanted to cry.

Mr Kirmani sighed.

"Time of death" … he glanced at his watch then at the clock as if to reassure himself that this was indeed the case, "22.59".

Chapter Seven

Now they were singing which although loud and painful, was better than belligerence, Tracy reasoned. And there were a lot of them. Typical poxy Saturday night kicking-out crowd, finished in the pubs, contemplating a takeaway but dropping in on A&E on the way for the mates who had fallen over/tripped/carved themselves up on drinking vessels/passed out/collided with fixed structures/sought shelter from the rain/argued with moving vehicles/fought with the enemy, perceived or real/needed a pee/decided to check out the totty in nurse's uniforms. Fronk was always such a disappointment in the main, but occasionally, a most pleasant surprise, not least to Fronk himself. Not that the pub patients were always male. The girls were less frequent visitors but no less enthusiastic and generally in a far worse condition, especially if they had been brawling with their own kind. On these occasions Tracy had usually to call for back up. The lads were loud and boisterous but could usually be bawled into submission. The girls fought like caged cats, spitting and hissing, scratching and biting. Acrylic nails were a particular hazard, especially when they were embellished. Tetanus injections were much in demand along with local anaesthetic when scratches had to be probed for lost ornamentation that had detached itself from source and come to rest within the opposition.

The diehards who had been waiting for hours were the most vocally discontented, highly resentful of the influx. Not enough seats, we've been here for hours, no better than they should be, what did they expect if they went out drinking? What did they think this was – a public convenience?

In many ways it was but Tracy refrained from saying so, or from commenting that they as tax payers were funding it. Some of the faces were familiar – regulars, on first name terms. They knew their way around the system and the department, availed themselves of the facilities, enquired about Tracy's health and how her week had been. The lopsided digital noticeboard was the source of much curiosity and when regaled about the road traffic accident within the department that had occurred earlier, they were deeply affected. Fascinated. Dawn found herself in the centre of attention and the catalyst for an animated discussion in which she had the loudest voice, the most experience and was the principal witness. It was thrilling. What, with the drama of Mrs Lewinski and the police presence earlier, it was almost enough to offset the disappointment of the appendix that had remained intact.

With the invading hordes came the rain, the noise and the vomit. Mostly on the men's shirts which bore testament to previous close encounters with toilet bowls and the street as their trousers made concerted efforts to escape the scene of the crime and tried to fall off their buttocks, taking their belts with them. Only their underpants – if they wore any – declared their loyalty and could be seen valiantly clinging onto rain drenched bottoms as trousers and belts made their way south. The girls, marginally less stained around the chest area compensated by the sparsity of their attire, to the great delight of the spectating audience. Most wore waterproof make up so flaunted perfect mask-faces above crop tops clinging limpet-like to underboobs above tiny pelmet skirts, struggling to contain cool, damp flesh. The skirts worked alone, without the assistance of underwear any more substantial than a thong. When this became apparent whenever they made any movement other than walking in a straight line, there was roar of male approval and even the waiting room itself seemed to be watching like some furtive voyeur. Shazza and Dawn would have liked to have been shocked but were too fascinated. Mrs Lewinski did not notice. The quantities of large carbohydrate-fuelled female belly rolling between crop tops and skirts were mesmerising, especially if any sign of a piercing could be detected peeping out from beneath shivery folded flesh.

Inspired no doubt by the sexually charged atmosphere of the room and the vast quantities of alcohol imbibed over the course of an evening out, Tracy became an object of great amorous interest to the male visitors. She was their first port of call on arrival – even they knew that they had first to check in at the reception desk before availing themselves of the facilities. It started immediately, as soon as they spotted her stuck behind the counter, unable to escape or run, thereby required to acknowledge, to listen and perhaps, joy of joys, even to make eye contact. This, beer goggles and their alcoholic fervour unleashed the most determined of the male chat up routines. All those one-liners cribbed from dating sites and self-help manuals then practised in front of mirrors or on lone dog walks found themselves coming up for air and being lobbed out into the open in the direction of the hapless receptionist. Alas, they fell on stony ground. Tracy was solid, fixed, impassive and immune. She looked at them, saw nothing and heard even less. A filter developed over years had attuned her brain to register only name, date of birth, contact details, reason for visit and to take a seat please. Waiting times are on the screen on the wall, toilets to the right. Who's next?

That was not to say she did not see what was happening in the room before her. The return of Mrs Lewinski to a seat to wait while her husband was treated had not gone unnoticed, nor the conversation with the two fat cows on either side of her. She had heard the words 'sue' and 'negligence' and was on high alert. Even as she processed the new comers, she kept Mrs Lewinski in her sights. So when Mr Kirmani appeared through the previously closed door and surveyed the room, Tracy knew exactly who he was looking for. In tow was Sister D, so it was obvious that the news was going to be of the worst kind. Tracy stroked a forearm, pressed her thighs together and reached for the Red Bull.

Mrs Lewinski had a name, Sonya, but no immediate relatives or friends to be with her so she received the news of her husband's death sitting quietly on the edge of a plastic chair in the same room that had witnessed the interview about Rohan's sexual assault (alleged). Mr Kirmani had delivered many such messages over the course of a long career but it was always dreadful. You never knew how the bereaved would react. He had seen it all, from hysterical laughter with violence to catatonic shock, but gentle sobbing was often the worst. There was just nothing you could say or do to alleviate the hopelessness. Suddenly Mrs Lewinski – Sonya as they now thought of her – was on her own, stranded in grief, cushioned perhaps for a while by shock but forced to accept that her husband had left her, and she had not even been able to say goodbye.

"I shouted at him." Her eyes were wide with disbelief shrouded by tears. "I shouted at him". Now she was talking to herself, horrified.

"I'm so sorry, Sonya. We did everything we could."

How feeble it sounded, and the consultant knew it. The bereaved woman looked at him.

"But he only hit his head on the kitchen cupboard. I don't understand."

In a way, nor did he. It was just one of those ghastly things. More often than not, a person slipped on a wet floor and at worst might break a limb or be bruised. Or they crossed the clear road and no car hit them at breakneck speed and broke every bone in their body. It happened.

"The injury caused bleeding on his brain and his heart just couldn't cope with the shock of the procedure to try and drain it."

If he was about to explain that they had to attempt the drain or Andrez would probably have died anyway, he decided against it.

Likewise, the damage to his brain even if the procedure had succeeded and the neurosurgeons had managed to stem the flow.

The weeping was now silent; tears trickled over her cheeks, stalled momentarily in the creases around her mouth then dripped off her face. Sister D handed her a tissue which she ignored.

"He's dead?"

So, she did realise. Sometimes the bereaved beloved had to have it spelled out to them; even though they heard the words, they did not understand, did not process the reality and then they could not begin to grieve and come to terms – if they ever fully did – with their loss. Mr Kirmani reached for her hand which he covered with his own, now gloveless. The latex gloves tainted with the death of her husband had been consigned to the incinerator, as he would soon be consigned to the morgue.

"I'm so sorry."

He really was. Andrez's death – anyone's death was always devastating. He had entered medicine to heal and it was only that optimism that had sustained him over the years. Death felt like failure; incompetence; professional betrayal and although he knew that there were times when it was inevitable, it did not help. Not so different to the bereaved he thought – I know the facts but can't accept the reality. Why do we always think we can save and cure? Who do we think we are? For a second, he would have liked to take the proffered tissue for himself but that would have been a double betrayal so he girded his consultant loins and straightened his dishevelled tie. God, he hadn't even had time to scrub up. They really had moved as fast and done as much as they could. It was what it was.

"But why did you send him home when he came in before? Why didn't you treat him then? If you had this wouldn't have happened and he wouldn't be dead."

The room felt very cold. Mr Kirmani stared at Sonya, now rapidly returning to Mrs Lewinski.

"I beg your pardon?"

It was his turn to be horrified. He looked at Sister D whose face was a mask. Both looked at the new widow.

"The receptionist sent him home. He didn't see anyone, not even a nurse. That's what they said out there." She indicated the waiting room with gesture so violent, so pronounced that the air in the stuffy room broke. "They saw it all. They told me."

Mr Kirmani's sorrow and regret disappeared to a distant point on a foreign horizon. This was an altogether different kind of nightmare. Any death on the premises was a serious incident that had to be investigated – SIRIs were a way of hospital life, that was accepted practice, deservedly so but…negligence? Failing in their duty of care?

"That is a very serious allegation, Mrs Lewinski."

"I won't be fobbed off" she replied, defiant, miraculously dry eyed. "My husband's dead and it's your fault."

It was fortunate that Graham Parsons was ascetic by both nature and taste; his office sported the very best of NHS economy. Functional sparse combined with shabby cheap would be the best way of describing his office. Some of his colleagues tried to soften and improve their work spaces but he felt no such need to introduce potted plants, desk tidies, lamps, family photographs and, horror of horrors, humorous calendars or those terrible ones with cutesy animals. He was always suspicious of staff who displayed such sentimentality; it suggested weakness, sloppiness of mind and body. More than once he had toyed with the notion of conducting research into the relationship between the overweight and their functionless domestic pets, living versions of stuffed toys. Some might call him fattist, but that was an oversimplification. He disapproved of the overweight not because he thought they were ugly, unpleasant or even unhealthy, but because it demonstrated a shocking lack of self-discipline, of self-control, self-respect even. However, he kept his views private and a strong sense of moral fair play made him treat everyone, regardless of size, with the same mathematical objectivity. He was a man who watched rather than shared; measured everything but made his calculations in private.

The situation with Rohan Patel was regrettable, very regrettable. Fortunately, the man had left the premises without demur and there was a certain perverse pleasure in sitting alone, sorting out the paperwork undisturbed, in his over-lit, under-furnished office. The Venetian blinds were drawn, a little unevenly which was annoying but unavoidable due to the nature of the cords, stiff and dark with age and exposure to the sun, that operated them. He had been offered new curtains, proper ones made of something lasting, when he was given the office but had refused. Really, there was no need and blinds were much less trouble: so much easier to clean. If only he could straighten them.

Having dealt with the Patel problem he decided to address his in-tray and take the opportunity to catch up on the very few things he had carried over from yesterday. It would give him a clear run on Monday morning and he would enjoy the feeling of going to church in the morning knowing that he had earned his seventh day. He liked the Sabbath. Even when on call and as a junior doctor it had felt different; there was a frisson of righteousness in working on what ought to be a day of rest which suited his sense of self-denial and service. So when the serenity of his peaceful office was fractured by the intrusion of his mobile, he was both surprised and irritated. He had not even put it onto silent. It had never occurred to him that anyone else would disturb him this evening. His wife was out, no doubt availing herself of the cheese board he had so sadly missed, but she knew better than to call him at work. He reached for the phone and frowned. Kirmani. What did he want? Hadn't he caused enough trouble already and he wasn't even an anaesthetist?

The septic butt cheek had been cleared, cleansed and closed. It presented a sadly deflated profile under the sterile sheet which unfortunately served only to emphasise the size and solidity of its recumbent partner. Clothing might indeed be a problem.

"Skirts?" offered the surgeon who was male.

The other theatre staff who were predominantly female raised eyebrows over sterile masks and pitied him his subsequent interview with the patient and her mother. Out in the waiting room the lively air of post-pub jollity continued. Alcohol scented the air, nuanced by stale cigarette smoke clinging to clothes with notes of takeaway, faintly exotic, spicy, oily and fried. So far, Tracy reasoned, so good. No vomiting or urinating in public spaces; much noise but little aggression; nothing she could not handle. She was a survivor and now had Red Bull in her veins. Her temporary discomposure had departed and she felt confident enough to peer out into the waiting room with her best don't-mess-with-me look and then to respond almost cheerfully to Fronk who had appeared behind her. He must be taking a breather, she thought. No time for a proper break but it was nice of him to pop by for a quick chat; it broke up the exhausting monotonous tension. Having asked her if she was okay, which was unexpected and rather sweet, he said he wanted her advice. This was also rather sweet and she leant back in her chair, as far as its rigidity and non-ergonomic form permitted. He was thinking of getting a tongue split – what did she think?

Her immediate reaction was why? who in their right mind? but she had sense enough not to say. It was all about personal expression apparently: individuality and self-perception. Body art was more than superficial decoration. It transcended gender, social mores, place and time – it had its roots in ancient cultures where people were more true to themselves, removed from the strictures of socialisation and cultural prejudice. He wanted to get back to his innate, pre-civilised roots. Also, he was going to a massive body art fair in Belgium where everybody would have one.

Tracy was thoughtful, mainly because she had absolutely no idea what to say. Then became inspired.

"What do the others say?"

Fronk looked a little disheartened. They had not been very encouraging, he admitted. Sister D. had asked why he wanted to speak with a forked tongue and what would it be next? Horns? Cloven feet and a tail? Mac had been more sympathetic but had really not needed to list all the potential medical problems caused by such a procedure and then top it off by asking how would he be able to lick things? Mr Kirmani was busy so had not been consulted but, to be honest, Fronk did not think he would understand at all. It wasn't really a consultant thing, body art but, here he brightened. Maybe, one day! He had heard there were already consultants with tattoos. And women pierced their ears, didn't they? Even Royalty. Tracy fingered her own multiple ear piercings of which she only ever used two; the rest that climbed up her ears towards her scalp had grown over and now looked like aging blackheads. It had been the fashion when she was young to rivet your ears like something off a military hardware production line but times change, and it had cost a fortune in earrings which, by necessity, had to be cheap and caused all sorts of discolouration and infection.

She was about to suggest that a tongue stud might be a more workable solution when she was distracted. The double doors had swept apart to reveal the shape of Dudley, in all his green muscled glory. He stood there for a moment, quite still, so that his Herculean form could be fully appreciated. Legs akimbo, shoulders back, stomach in and chest out, it was quite ten seconds before they realised that he was supporting another body with one brawny outstretched arm. The body, which appeared to be male, was folded over the stretcher like a tea towel badly in need of washing. It hung, limp and damp, as slack and soft and pliable as Dudley was not.

It was Rohan. Dudley wheeled the anaesthetist into the room. Plump, squidgy and soft like some oversized cuddly toy on a shelf he was completely unresponsive. He was also extremely wet. One arm dripped rainwater morosely over the side of the trolley and swung in time with Dudley's marching pace. His paramedic colleague had stayed outside for a quick smoke – a habit Dudley abhorred and could not bear to witness so he had undertaken the task of delivering the patient, whom he knew, although more by reputation than in the flesh. Nevertheless, he felt a responsibility. Dudley often felt responsibilities, even when they weren't there. At the reception desk he stopped, presented arms and smartly brought the trolley to a halt. There was a groan, a deep-seated gargle and Rohan opened his mouth. He retched with such violence that his body seemed to dance, horizontally, like a snake trying to digest an overlarge and awkwardly shaped lunch. He thrashed and coiled, straightened, then coiled again. Would have fallen off the trolley if Dudley had not kept restraining arms on him. This was repeated, with the assistance of gravity from his elevation, with throaty gags, gasps, primeval coughs, splashes and more gargles. Eventually it was over - everything: the Please Wait Your Turn area in front of the counter, Dudley's ex-army boots, the NHS issue floor tiles (who had seen it all before) and, increasingly, in a fast flowing stream aiming for the mesmerised spectators who all involuntarily leant back in their seats like an audience watching a performing whale. Dudley found himself surrounded by a lake of stringy vomit and drool like a statue stranded in a pool of classical dimensions. Rohan was immobile again, but moaning softly.

"He's drunk."

Tracy gaped and tried not to mind the stench.

"He doesn't drink."

"He does now."

They both stared at the former abstainer, forbidden by his religion to consume stimulating substances such as alcohol and famously even circumspect about the effect of coffee.

"I found him in the street. Outside the off license."

"He's soaked."

"It's raining. He was in the gutter."

They both looked some more while Rohan groaned, as if to protest his innocence.

"Someone rang 999. He's lucky he got me!"

Debatable, but whatever he was, had done, or would become, Rohan was one of their own, at least for the moment.

"I'll get Sister D…no, Fronk." Tracy sighed and reached for the phone. "The porter'll have to be called. Hell. It's Kolya tonight and you know what he's like."

By now the smell of whisky-soured vomit was pervasive, reaching all corners and curves of the waiting area and enthusiastically making forays into the corridors beyond. Soon it would reach Kolya himself and he would know exactly what was afoot; Tracy had to alert him before the smell did or life would be even more unbearable. Kolya had a way of not speaking that destroyed confidence, slayed the opposition and inspired reverential fear throughout the hospital. She braced herself and reached for the phone.

Fronk was magnificent. By the time Kolya had been appraised of 'the situation' – no one ever summoned him; they would not dare - Rohan had been lifted into the hallowed recesses of the treatment room and laid to rest on his side in a cubicle 'to sleep it off' under observation. He had been undressed and clammy abundant flesh was now swaddled in a couple of NHS gowns, tied wherever possible and resembling an informal, gaily patterned strait jacket. His privileged position of being 'one of them' had prompted Fronk to set up a drip so that a steady influx of non-alcoholic fluid would help to dilute, swill out and hydrate the maiden drunk. Not much they would be able to do about the hangover and inevitable self-recrimination to follow but he would get over it; they always did. In the waiting room, the drunks were quieter than usual and a few even stumbled to the exit and disappeared, carefully avoiding eye contact with Tracy as they departed.

"Oh well" said Fronk when he reappeared to update Tracy on Rohan's condition. "At least his wife won't know."

"Whaddya mean?"

Tracy was struggling with the knowledge that there was indeed a Mrs Patel and how in the hell could she not know what her beloved spouse had been up to?

"She'll think he's still at work. His shift hasn't finished yet."

"Will you speak to her, or shall I?" Graham Parsons was consulting with the consultant. Mr Kirmani already knew the answer and the protocol, but it was nice to be asked. Parsons was good like that – a cold fish but irreproachably polite.

"I will, of course. But only as a preliminary. HR need to be in on this. She's admin, not medical."

"That, I think, is the crux of the problem" the Medical Director sourly pointed out.

Chapter Eight.

Midnight. The witching hour. Or was that just Kolya? Tracy could not decide but thankfully did not have to. As she was discreetly watching the porter her reverie was interrupted by someone clearing their throat. A young man stood before her, accompanied by an equally young woman with pain in her eyes. They were standing: he erect, she slightly bent forward, legs apart. No one spoke. Tracy took the initiative and, with as much interest as she could muster at that time of night and in the presence of Kolya, asked if she could help. Clearly she succeeded; the young man answered with a kind of desperate earnestness that spoke for them both. His name was Jordan -he put himself first Tracy noticed – then identified the woman as his girlfriend, Shelley. Surnames were not offered so Tracy decided not to ask, not yet. The expression on Shelley's face seemed to suggest that it was more important to get to the reason for their visit.

Could Tracy help? Yes, yes, he – they – hoped so. Very much. So, what was the problem?

"We've lost our car keys."

It was with great difficulty that Tracy maintained a polite exterior as she fought with a surge of irritation that came deep from within. 'When in doubt, throw it back at them' usually worked and would stall the conversation almost long enough for her to regain some level of professional composure.

"You've lost your key cars?"

"Yes" A vigorous nodding of the head from him and a narrowing of the eyes from her. Pain had given way to a cat-like gleam.

"You know that this is a hospital, right?"

"Oh yes" More nodding of the head. Much more and with a bit of luck it'll drop off Tracy thought.

"Not the AA?"

"We know that" cat's eyes said with a warning hiss. Tracy got the message. Jordan did not. He continued.

"We know where they are, but we can't get them, if you know what I mean."

By now those in the front rows, having survived the onslaught of vomit closely followed by the life-sucking silence of Kolya, were ready for a diversion and with the guile of school children scenting an inexperienced teacher, were ready to pounce. They sat perfectly still, concentrating, also leaning slightly forward as if in sympathy with Shelley, all the better to hear.

No. Tracy didn't know what they meant. She had an idea but kept that to herself. Perhaps they'd like to be more explicit?

Shelley obviously did not but Jordan sailed on, oblivious to the decreasing temperature and increasing boisterousness of the waves.

"Well…" he considered for a moment. "They're inside…her ... and we can't get them out."

Dawn extended a podgy arm and poked Shazza with a very dimpled elbow. Both were smiling – guessing – speculating – loving every second – begging that it became more salacious. All the signs were there. Tracy became cruel.

"You've swallowed them?"

Shelley's eyes were now slits. Dark, fathomless and furious. She would have drowned Jordan if she could but he persisted in staying afloat, just.

"In a manner of speaking. Sort of up from below rather than down from the top, if you get my drift?"

Dawn, Shazza and everyone else within earshot immediately focused delighted attention on the top of Shelley's straddled legs and sighed with satisfaction. How nice to have expectations met! Possibly even exceeded. They all settled back to enjoy in as much comfort as NHS waiting room chairs could afford.

Over-arching over-plucked eyebrows reaching for her greasy pie-bald fringe, Tracy assumed a perfect receptionist persona and pressed on. She focused on Jordan in case he went under. Would Shelley like to take a seat?

"No." She would rather stand, thank you. Fine, she could suit herself, Tracy shrugged; it was all the same to her.

"I need a description of the keys as well as where, when and how. So that they know what they're looking for. Name and date of birth?"

"Volkswagen Polo. 2016"

Dawn choked. Shazza laughed so hard she nearly swallowed herself before hammering her friend on the back with such violence that they both wobbled and rocked.

"I meant your girlfriend."

Tracy failed to convince anyone that her giggle was a foreign body in her throat that had to be cleared. She so wanted to laugh but did not dare; more than her job was worth.

"Who'll cover reception while we interview her?" Graham Parsons asked Mr Kirmani. It was vital that everything continued to run smoothly. The government target maximum A&E waiting time of four hours had already been shot to pieces and lay bleeding, badly mutilating the monthly hospital statistics spreadsheet. Such heinous savagery of Dept of Health guidelines could possibly be justified by unprecedented medical emergencies but the removal of a member of admin staff would not look good, especially when they were already running so far behind. "Is there anyone on site who can stand in for her?"

Mr Kirmani shook his head. They were not a centre of excellence, on 24/7 high alert and fully staffed night and day. This was Wyeminster – they were lucky to be able to operate an all-night A&E at all and their existence only continued because there was nowhere else for miles. Really serious cases were transferred to other more specialised centres, usually in Birmingham and occasionally Bristol. Certainly, that is what would have happened to Andrez Lewinski if he had survived. Sometimes, Mr Kirmani thought, it felt as if they were little better than a field hospital, patching up the injured. The walking wounded could be discharged to return at a later date while the really sick were stabilised for survival then shipped out to more sophisticated facilities elsewhere.

"I suggest we wait until later, when things ease off a bit - once the closing time crowd have been put through. Then we can talk to her properly."

"We don't seem to have much alternative" the Medical Director said gloomily, resigned now to a long night without a cheeseboard. "Call me when she's available. I'll be in my office."

To Shelley's great relief but not yet physical comfort, Fronk was prompt in calling them through for assessment. His cheerfulness was offensive but not half as mortifying as his analysis.

"Shelley? This way. … Easy does it…. Inadvertent rectal object?"

She said nothing but Jordan – bloody Jordan –chose to concur and then engaged in conversation and the two men started chatting. Chatting! She was outraged. A nurse that looked like a freak discussing her predicament with the perpetrator of her agony and shame.

"How did you get here?" the freak was asking. "By taxi?"

Damn it. Now they were discussing the cost and availability of taxis as opposed to public transport during anti-social hours. She wanted to kill them both but could hardly walk, so maiming was not even an option. Instead she seethed as noisily as she could and shuffled furiously into the cubicle pointed out to her, but neither noticed. At least the nurse, who went by a highly improbable name which he had no doubt assumed to match his equally improbable appearance, offered her his hand to help clamber onto the bed. Jordan, she noticed with rage, stood back and continued talking. They had moved onto the subject of cars. She swore to herself, glimmered dangerous stiletto thin black pupils at her beloved and vowed revenge.

After a brief consultation Fronk, who had not even examined her, left them alone in the cubicle while he went off to get some doctor or other, she wasn't really listening.

"How could you? How could you be so bloody stupid?"

Cat's eyes shimmered and she spat out the words. Jordan's eyes in turn opened wide and his face was cherubic, innocent, astonished. Hadn't it been her idea? They were the nearest thing to hand. He'd only done what she'd wanted. It wasn't his fault. How could she even suggest it? Fortuitously at that moment Mac swung the blushing curtain aside to make the acquaintance of the couple with the keys-up-the-arse otherwise Jordan's injuries might have further added to the unacceptably long wait currently faced by all those in A&E.

The Australian accent had just begun to introduce itself when it was crushed, strangled at birth by the magnitude of the hissing outside the cubicle curtain. Sister D. had been religiously checking her department, as she did, very often and had discovered Rohan. Fronk had been summoned to explain himself. In the tradition of the best stage whisper when everyone heard, from proscenium arch to the Gods, she began the interrogation.

"What's he doing here?" Metaphorically clutching Fronk by one airy ear lobe and shaking him like an errant school boy she fixed him with the wither look.

"Sleeping it off."

"He doesn't drink."

"He does now."

"He can't stay here. Not after what he's done."

"He can't go home like that."

Even Shelley was listening raptly, consoled by the knowledge that other people had problems. Not that that excused Jordan. She looked at him with poison in her eyes and would gladly have spoken with forked tongue at that moment, even if it did mean looking like Fronk. Mac gave a thespian cough and the hissing abruptly stopped. A swift foot shuffle and the whisper receded enough for the trio behind the curtain to hear more only if they concentrated.

"He's suspended. That means he can't be on hospital premises, Fronk. He has to go."

"But he's completely out of it. He can't even walk."

A bulky sigh, the full capacity of Sister D's commodious lungs and a concession was made. Alright, he could stay – as a patient only, mind – until he was well enough to be discharged and then he was to be escorted from the premises and absolutely not, - do you hear me? - not to be allowed back or contacted thereafter by anyone in the department. Was that clear? And it would be better for everyone (she stamped both feet on the word for emphasis) if his presence was not made general knowledge, especially as the Medical Director (sniff of derision) was on the premises (when he should be at home minding his own business). Fronk was dismissed. Mac tried to pretend that what they had just heard had never happened.

"Okay! Shelley isn't it? Hi I'm Dr Mackenzie but they all call me Mac. So, you have a set of car keys in your back passage?"

They would need to be removed, obviously. He assumed that Jordan had tried to get them out? He had. Shelley's face confirmed this without words and suggested also that the attempts had been far from either comfortable or beneficial. Would Shelley mind if he took a quick look? Great! That's it, on your side or maybe you could crouch on all fours with your face towards the wall…? Lovely… Yes, there was definitely something there but it was quite difficult to see. They would send her for an X-ray to find out exactly how the keys were placed and then take it from there. As it were. Only Shelley did not snigger. Hopefully the keys would not be too far out of reach so extraction would be relatively simple, assuming that they were not awkwardly positioned. It was important to remove them vertically, not horizontally if you see what I mean? Don't want to do any damage do we? He would go and organise an X ray asap and meanwhile, perhaps they'd like to stay in the cubicle instead of in the waiting room? The chairs there were rather hard and it might be a bit uncomfortable. From her crouching position all Shelley needed was fur to be fully feline. Gimlet eyed she turned herself over onto her side and flicked her tail with fury.

"I won't split."

"Yer what?"

"My tongue. I'll pierce. Like you say. Or maybe my cheek. I know of a guy with holes in his cheeks – you make them the same way as the ears."

Tracy peered through the rimmed orifices adorning Fronk's neck.

"How d'you eat? Wouldn't they leak?"

"You plug them."

Tracy visualised two sink plugs in Fronk's visage and wondered if you would have to have metal ball chains to stop them falling in or, indeed, for pulling them out. Perhaps he would attach them to his ears?

"Easy to clean your teeth I s'pose" she said doubtfully. "Get to all those fiddly bits at the back."

"I hadn't thought of that!" Fronk beamed. "Thanks Trace. You're a pal. Need more paracetamol yet?"

Tracy's ongoing ailments, aches, pains and suffering were old friends to everyone in the department. Even the relatively new Sister D had been introduced, although she kept her distance, as she did with all relationships. Boundaries! It was all about boundaries. That was the problem today: people did not respect boundaries and everything was getting out of control. The world was being held hostage to expediency. And celebrities. She had never herself supplied Tracy with pain killers from the drugs trolley and of course, never would, but she knew that it went on. Most of the staff were at it. Headaches, hangovers, PMT, incipient colds and sore throats – stupid to buy over the counter drugs when there they were, in abundance, on every drugs trolley in every ward in all the world. They worked for the NHS for God's sake! Which was worse? A couple of paracetamols or taking the day off? And yes, they had a point so Sister D pretended not to know and the department ran on its merry way.

Yes please, that would be very nice – thank you. Tracy actually smiled. Oooh, a coffee would be lovely to wash it down, if he was offering? Fronk was an angel. Had he ever thought of entering one of the caring professions? Ha Ha! Very funny and Fronk had gone, head full of flesh-eating holes of ever-increasing dimensions, in pursuit of drugs and caffeine for the lovely Tracy whom he really quite liked and would simply love to do a make-over on. Especially that hair. Something like that he thought as he passed a girl entering through the tireless double doors. Her hair was deadly nightshade-purple, seamless, flat and glossy. It swung around a face like a damaged mushroom – white and smudged, heavily etched with black eyeliner and bruise-black lips where the mushroom had been pinched and squeezed. She wore Goth like a badge: a new recruit: white snowflake lost in the dark. Black pseudo Victorian boots laced to the knee, opaque black tights, the tiniest of tiny tartan skirts below a meticulously torn black T shirt, carefully ironed into a casual stretch tight around her girl-woman chest and frayed with tweezers. The fungoid face was streaky and uneven where the eyeliner had slipped and dribbled, as if someone had tried to cut the mushroom with a spoon.

At the reception desk she looked at Tracy for a second, said nothing, then started to snivel. Snot began to edge towards the black edged lips which she wiped on the sleeve of her denim jacket with an upward swipe so as to address the source of the problem. Then she stood, wiping her snotty sleeve against her the side of her jacket and looked beseechingly at the disgusted receptionist.

"Yes?" Tracy sniffed almost as loudly as the sticky Goth before her and studied the glistening snail trail adhering to the denim.

"I dunno what to do."

Tracy sniffed critically, sighed and started to speak.

"Why're you here?"

The girl who looked all of thirteen, came a little closer to the counter and began to fiddle with the hem of her T shirt which she lifted up to just below her girl-woman breasts. She was not wearing any discernible underwear and for a moment Tracy feared full scale nipple exposure, but mercifully the girl desisted before NHS dress codes were breached. Mushroom face reconsidered, mid-midrift, then lowered her top. Before Tracy could utter a word, she began to disrobe from the top down, slipping off her jacket and easing one hollow-clavicle shoulder out of the T shirt so that her left protuberance – too small to be called a breast but too big to be flat chested – was almost bare. But not quite, those in the waiting room noticed, with mixed feelings. What was evident however, to all those (everyone) who looked, was that the word 'Chayse' was written in large, uneven black Gothic script across the hitherto concealed virgin flesh.

"What's Chayse?" Tracy asked.

"My bastard boyfriend."

Buttocks shifted and settled on the front row for increased comfort.

"Ex I assume?"

"Yeah. Bastard."

"That's as maybe. But why're you here?"

"I wanna get rid of it."

Tracy looked. Dawn, Shazza, most of the others on the front row and some of the drunks also looked, but perhaps the latter were more focused on the fried egg breast that lay tantalisingly out of view just below the line of fabric on the exposed chest.

"Why get it done then?"

The Goth/mushroom roared into action. She'd only got it done three days ago because she was so tote in love with Chayse, know what I mean? No, Tracy didn't; she had more sense. The fledgling Goth was not surprised. No, she understood, for reals. Must be crap being old.

Silence.

Tracy asked her why, if she loved him so much, she wanted Chayse removed. Three days! Obviously a long term relationship?

The bruise lips pouted and pursed and the clumsy kohl eyes were stones – the first real thing about her face.

"My best mate went to bed with him. Bitch."

"Watch your language" Tracy replied, playing the Mum card. Fledgling Goth apologised and became tearful. The mushroom looked as if it had been put into a hot pan and was about to soften and disintegrate.

"Chayse wanted to, y'know, do the whole sex thing but I said no coz' tbh I don't think I'm into that so Chantelle the Ho went with him and I hate them both they've broken my heart and now I've got this, this THING " – she jabbed at her broken heart "on me and that's why I gotta get rid of it…."

Tracy and the waiting room contemplated this tale of woe. Certainly she seemed pathetic but that might have been because the snowflake was starting to melt.

And why did she think it was an emergency? Tracy wanted to know. Saturdays, especially late at night on Saturdays, in case she did not realise, were part of weekends which meant that they were not weekdays so it was emergencies only. Why couldn't she go to her GP (another word for your own doctor, love) on Monday? Or Tuesday? Or any other day that wasn't the weekend or anything to do with the Wyeminster, A&E and most important of all, Tracy?

"Duh, he's just posted a picture of me on Snapchat."

Now the tears really started to flow, carving their way through the sickly foundation like fingers through wet paint.

"And my parents don't know about it and if they find out they'll kill me."

"Before or after your heart gives up?" Tracy knew she would have to, albeit, reluctantly return to the more orthodox script of her profession but she was enjoying herself. "This isn't an emergency and there's nothing we can do to help. Unless you have a heart attack, of course."

The wet paint was drying, the finger tracks halted, the tears no more.

"Whaddya mean?" Goth was on her high horse. Snowflake had rights and meant to get them.

"This is an accident and emergency department. You haven't had an accident and a tattoo of a scumbag boyfriend is not an emergency. So, we can't help you. Next please."

Goth found herself dismissed, elbowed aside, replaced by an anxious mother and father carrying a spotty child with crimson cheeks. But the battle was not over, and she did not leave but quietly positioned herself out of Tracy's view and began to thumb her phone with a rapidity and adeptness known only to Millennials.

The waves went in and out. Shelley – 'the one with the keys up her you know where' - was seen to shuffle off not her mortal coil but to X ray, Dawn surmised. That'd give 'em a much-needed laugh on a Saturday night, eh Shazza? Sunday morning Shazza said and readjusted her buttocks. It was indeed, a long wait, but so exciting and although emergencies, obviously, they were not that urgent so could afford to sit back and enjoy themselves. The drunks were processed, urinated (mostly in the toilet bowls) and had stopped singing as the sedative effect of excess imbibing began to take effect. Like Rohan, slumbering peacefully on paper sheets behind a disposable curtain, they began to fall asleep where they sat/perched/lay on the floor like over-sized hairy babies. With every appearance in the waiting room Fronk smiled a little more as he watched the waiting hordes reduce in both size and volume. Sleeping it off: cheap, readily available, drug free and independent of trained medical NHS personnel. Perhaps they should have dormitories? Kolya had disappeared so Tracy could relax and she even managed to drink some of the coffee Fronk had delivered, even if it was from the machine and cold.

"My name's Skylar Blue Brooke and I require emergency treatment."

Tracy looked up – or rather down at the voice on the other side of the counter. Damn. She thought she recognised it. The Goth was standing there, phone in one hand and attitude in the other. Eyes narrowed; assume position; ready, aim, fire.

"You again".

"Yeah. I've got…" Goth glanced down at her phone "cellulitis."

"Since when?"

"Cellulitis is a potentially serious bacterial skin infection. It.." She consulted her phone … "occurs when certain types of bacteria enter the skin through a cut or a crack. Like a tattoo". Suck that up bitch her face said. Tracy sucked, tasted the foulness but had form.

"I know about cellulitis. Your tattoo looked alright to me."

"Are you a doctor?"

Ouch. No, she wasn't. Goth smirked. Tracy surrendered.

They began the age-old sign them in and put them on the system routine, Tracy with a face like a squeezed lime, Skylar Blue Brooke, date of birth 20 April 2007, grinning …

"Hang on. You're only 13."

WTF Skylar sighed.

"Told the tattoo parlour you were sixteen, did you?"

"None of your business" Goth grinned so Tracy registered her as Skylark Flue Brooke.

"Take a seat, Skylark" she said, "and wait for the someone to come and assess you. Shouldn't take long" she added, but whether she meant the wait or the assessment was not clear.

Jordan escorted his lover back to her bed of pain and there they waited in thorny silence for Mac to deliver his verdict. He was infuriatingly upbeat which really pissed off Shelley and she said so. But, like her dearly beloved, the Down Under doctor appeared immune to her charms as he outlined their options.

"The good news is that the keys aren't that far up the rectum so we can remove them without too much difficulty. You can either be admitted and we can do it under a general anaesthetic or we can do it now. It's up to you."

Jordan was about to speak but got caught in the crossfire from Shelley's eyes so refrained. She was glaring at Mac, or whatever he called himself.

"Will it hurt if you do it now?"

"There'll be some discomfort, yes, but you'll be in theatre and as long as the keys come out vertically it shouldn't be too bad."

Shelley groaned and glared at Jordan who smiled, warily, as at a child eyeing up a nurse's hand before an injection.

"It's your call, Shel, but if we're going to drive the car … He drifted into silence and inhaled, exhaled sorrowfully, shrugged and adopted a forlorn expression which rendered him more apathetic than appealing. The cat's eyes lined themselves up for attack as they considered for a moment or two, then focused on Jordan who stood his ground. Mac watched with fascination but prepared to move at any second to avoid catching the crossfire: blue on blue. But Jordan knew his woman and although Shelley hated herself, even as she spoke, she gave her assent.

"Not that I'm doing this for you" she spat. "There's just no way I'm being admitted. How the hell would we explain it?" She turned to Mac, venom now spiced with suspicion. "What're you going to do?"

"We'll use a rigid sigmoidoscope…"

"A rigid what?"

Mac backtracked – too much detail too soon. The poor girl had clearly done with all things rigid for the time being. He described the instrument that they were proposing to insert up her rectum as if it was some sort of cuddly toy:

"It's like a short telescope with a light at the end. Nothing to be afraid of; very routine."

He wanted to say that they used them all the time but that, perhaps was more detail than strictly required in the current circumstances. Briefly he debated whether or not to entertain them with a description of strange objects he had found within back passages; Jordan would certainly appreciate the humour but doubts about Shelley made him decide to stay quiet. Strictly professional he thought, or keep it for the pub. She doesn't seem the sort to be amused. Shame though. They were great stories and all true. Even the one about the shower head and the light bulb.

"It blows air into the lower rectum and then we'll hopefully be able to see the keys and grab them and pull them out. Simples. This way" he breezed as Shelley eased herself off the bed and began waddling after him. Jordan offered her his arm but she batted it off like a wasp.

Fronk and Skylar were deep in conversation. He loved her hair and her boots; she adored his ear lobes. Oh, if only she was old enough to go to a Body Art Fair in Belgium but no, she hadn't even done her GCSEs. Hadn't even made her choices and didn't even know if she cared enough to bother. What did he mean she had to? Well how did she think he was doing this job if he didn't have qualifications? It took time and dedication to get ear lobes like his; it didn't just happen you know. It was all about the vision, the planning, small beginnings and persistence. Sometimes pain even, but that was par for the course. Just like passing GCSEs. And if she worked hard at school and did well, then her parents wouldn't be so mardy, would they? And why a tattoo? No man was worth that – believe me, he knew. The hospital couldn't remove it now or even later. It would have to be lasered and that would cost, far more than the tattoo itself. Maybe she could change the name to Chayste or something – it'd be easy to squeeze in a 't' with a sort of artistic squiggle and then her parents could hardly complain about self-proclaimed chastity, could they?

When she left, mollified, thoughtful and madly in love with all nurses with discs in their ears – she even smiled and waved at Tracy on the way out – Skylar had already vowed to put foolish things, like lads, behind her.

In theatre Shelley had been stripped and gowned. Standing in her faded NHS robe which did not seal at the back because it had lost its ties, she contemplated the structure before her with grim determination. Much as she now regarded her boyfriend. Jordan had done little to ease her discomfort by announcing that it didn't matter if the gown was open because that's the way the doc would have to go in anyway, so what were the odds? The doctor's Aussie injunction to 'just hop onto the table' also struck her as misplaced; she could not walk, never mind bloody hop. She did not care that it was called a Ritter table and was specially designed for easy access and good visibility in the parts where the sun failed to shine. However, she did as she was bid, and then it just got worse.

"Now if you could just lie on your side …that's it … now if you could pull up your knees towards your chin…a bit higher …

Lovely. I'm going move the table now so that we can tilt you up – a bit like a jack knife and that means I can get a better view…just like…that. Beautiful!"

Was it the table buzzing as it moved or Shelley spitting? Jordan wasn't sure but stood well back, just in case. Besides he too had a clearer view up Shelley's arse and it really was quite fascinating – he'd had no idea. Couldn't see the keys but it was surprisingly roomy up there. Who'd have guessed?

"Perfect! You're a natural Shelley" Mac enthused. "Okay, so now I'm just going to lubricate you then I'll insert the scope. Don't want it to stick, do we? Hold Jordan's hand if it helps."

Shelley would rather die in a cellar full of rats, thank you, than touch Jordan. This was all his bloody fault. She didn't know why she stuck with him the inconsiderate, self-centred …suddenly there was a huge gasp as she realised that the sigmoidoscope, in all its rigidity had embarked on its journey of discovery and was working its lubricated way up her very alarmed back passage. Not only had it been invaded by a set of Volkswagen Polo keys but now, as if that wasn't enough, some sort of tube had come calling and both of them uninvited.

"Try to relax, Shelley" Mac urged.

Shelley's outrage knew no bounds. Relax? In whose world? Wasn't that what Jordan had said and look where it had got her. Slippery suction noises filled the room; something akin to a greedy child sucking on an ice lolly in the process of melting mixed with the sniffing of someone desperately in need of tissue with which to blow a very snotty nose.

"Try not to clench" Mac encouraged.

"Urgh" Shelley replied and clenched. Mac was being as gentle as he could but had to make it clear to the reluctant rectum that resistance was useless so exerted more pressure and the scope proceeded steadily, steadily, into the darkness, its light shining like a miniature miner's lamp pinned to the helmet of the scope.

"Deep breath Shelley, that's it." The scope slid upwards and onwards with sudden gusto, as if fuelled by the intake of oxygen. Now groans and moans of outraged humiliation filled the air, tangoing with the sucking slipping sounds from within the inner recesses of Shelley's back passage.

"Wow!" Jordan joined in, percussion duetting with the wind section. "I can see right up your arse Shelley." Without waiting for her response, he pressed on, unaware that discretion was invariably the better part of valour. "Look! It's on the screen. In colour! … There are the keys!"

There they were indeed. In colour, as he had said. Shelley could not look – she was facing the wrong way and had not the slightest inclination to survey the contents of her own posterior, in colour or even monochrome and especially not in grossly magnified form on what sounded to her like a flat screen TV. She concentrated on deep breathing, like her sister had done in ante-natal classes when she had been expecting her first child. She hadn't bothered after that – the second and third babies just seemed to find their own way out and she simply did not have time to visit the supermarket never mind ante-natal classes. Having seen her sister's stretch marks and luggage laden eyes once she had become a mother, Shelley had resolved never to go down the same route and this experience had made her even more determined. Yes, it was different, in significant ways and obviously car keys did not count as producing offspring in any way at all, but the principle was the same. How could something the size of a baby, especially her nephew who had pitched up the size of an American quarterback's shoulders, ever make it down a birth canal and not cause utter devastation? Besides, to have a baby meant to get pregnant and there was no way she was ever having sex again, with anyone, especially Jordan. She glared, not at him because he was behind her but at the wall opposite and tried to distract herself from the machinations up her bottom by mentally castrating him with a selection of increasingly blunt objects.

Mac the irrepressible was enjoying himself. It was all going so well. He attempted to share his enthusiasm with the patient by giving her a running commentary. Such a pity she could not see the screen but Jordan would no doubt tell her all about it later; patients were generally discouraged from watching the procedure in case it upset or frightened them. She was not frightened though, was she? Not a marvellous patient like her; pity they weren't all like that. They were doing great and he could see the keys, all nicely vertical as if waiting to be collected. Couldn't wait to get out of there, as it were. They would come out as they went in … all he had to do was get hold of them and he was going to use a Spencer Wells forceps to do that. Lovely little instrument the Spencer Wells. … that was it … just one more little tug and … bingo! There was a plop as the keys emerged with a pitiful mew and they hung limp and wet, gasping for air, blinking in the sudden light. The scope followed with a slurp, licking itself clean and then there was an explosive fart as Shelley's rectum bid farewell to its uninvited guests. It blew a very moist fulsome raspberry which resonated around the room, bouncing off the metal surfaces from ceiling to floor, shaking itself dry like a wet dog.

Shelley was mortified. Would this humiliation never end?

"No worries, Shelley" Dr Mac consoled. "Happens all the time. Lots more to come after the amount the air we've blown up there. But worth it to get the keys out, eh? You can make yourself more comfortable now while I get someone to clean these for you." And he had gone, slimy keys in latex gloved hand, leaving Jordan to face the music.

Chapter Nine

Graham Parsons was resisting the urge to become irked – not irritated; he never permitted himself to be irritated – so bourgeois. But really, how long was this going to take? Surely it was possible to interview the woman by now? After all, it was only a preliminary interview, ostensibly to establish her view of events, but more significantly, to appraise her of Mrs Lewinski's allegations. And it could not be denied that they were very serious allegations which would have to be investigated internally and, God forbid, externally, if there was found to be any substance to them. He thought with regret of lost cheese and was ashamed to find himself feeling resentful; atonement would be required, especially as it was now – he glanced at his watch – the Sabbath Day. He would not eat until the following morning as penance and his heart leapt with guilty joy. He loved that feeling of being purged by hunger.

However he resolved to seek out Kirmani in his A&E lair without warning which would not only hopefully create an opportunity for the interview ('discussion' might be better in the first instance he decided) but would enable him to see for himself how the department coped under the stress and chaos that they claimed was a Saturday night. Personally, he had doubts. Stress and chaos were states of mind; circumstantial; entirely avoidable under competent management and well-rehearsed procedures. The inept could always find something to blame rather than their own inadequacies – lack of resources, lack of staff, unreasonable expectations that informed deadlines, the patients. When all that was required was proper leadership. He had always had misgivings about Kirmani and had heard the rumours about the goings on in A&E. Gossip he despised but rumours usually had some factual foundation to them so were worth listening to, but let it be known that he always waited until they reached him. He had to be above suspicion so chose to sit alone in the canteen, engrossed in an ostentatiously important document which repelled boarders, giving him cover to listen in on the conversations around him.

Knowing that his office lights would be visible from outside the building, he left them on as he closed the door and padded stiff-backed down the silent corridor towards A&E. His arrival would be all the more unexpected.

"Good as new" Mac said as he handed the Polo keys to Jordan. "We've washed them, thoroughly, for you. They've had quite an evening … as have you" he said noticing Shelley who was standing more upright but no less incandescent beside the bed. Jordan jangled the keys gratefully.

"Thanks Doc. Now I'll be able to go paintballing. It's this afternoon and was looking dodgy for a bit. But now I won't have to pay for a taxi or bum a lift and I'm good to go." Mac dared not look at the keys' previous incumbent but wondered how long it would be before either Jordan reappeared in A&E or the police were summoned to his abode by neighbours concerned about a domestic dispute.

The appearance of the medical director in A&E passed unnoticed; he was just one more shabby almost-senior citizen wandering around the place, probably looking for a toilet or the coffee machine or on his way to or from Imaging. The thin paper file clutched in his hand suggested that he was a lost out patient, desperately seeking something, somewhere. 'Not quite with it' was the general view as he shuffled along the rows of seats inspecting the occupants before he slid into the treatment area. Neither Dawn nor Shazza even noticed him so absorbed were they in the departure of the keys-no-longer-up-the-arse couple who had been forced to ring for a taxi from the direct link phone on the other side of the reception desk. Jordan had been swinging the keys jauntily from one finger in celebratory style until Shelley batted them out of his hand onto the floor. Then she made him pick them up and put them in his pocket, vowing never to touch them - or him - again.

Rohan had passed from dehydrated and sodden into pleasantly warm, a little moist and deeply asleep, lying on his back now, breathing heavily and snuffling like an overfed rabbit. His gowns had rearranged themselves in artistic folds and were draped across his belly, fluttering ever so slightly with every breath like gentle wings curled around his form. His knees, surprisingly hair free and knuckly were reclining in their sockets above perfectly relaxed hairy shins and ankles; his feet were turned out at ten-to-two and all was well with his world. Even the hairs on toes slumbered peacefully below the yellow nails that curled tenderly over the end of each toe. Unfortunately, the cherubic quality of this posture was somewhat compromised by the splayed legs from beneath the gown, which in its eagerness to cover the generous abdomen, had had to abandon the genital area. Rohan's assets were revelling in this new found freedom, light and (relatively) fresh air. They shivered and bounced upward with as much flaccid energy as they could muster with every inhalation then shuddered back into position with the subsequent exhalation. So much nicer than being kept in the dark. They would have waved in greeting if they could, especially to someone as eminent as the Medical Director.

Greeted first by quiescent genitalia, the MD was even more taken aback by the face he found at the top of the torso. He had to lean over the protruding abdomen to make sure it really was who he thought it was, then actually remove his glasses and wipe them before peering over the lenses for confirmation. It was not as if the man was even trying to be discreet – the cubicle curtain was not fully drawn: an open invitation. Flagrant. Debauched. Had the man no shame? And what in the name of all that was holy was he doing here? Stepping outside the cubicle he cast around for someone to annihilate. Sister D hove into view with Fronk trotting obediently at her side, to heel, prepared to do anything for a biscuit. Their erstwhile boss expected them to stop when they saw him but was disarmed by the unbroken pace of their continued progress. Eventually they did halt, mainly because he had placed himself directly in their path in the somewhat confined space so they would have had to diverge and wheel to avoid him.

"Yes?" Sister D looked at the clock on the wall as she barked. He might be the Medical Director but this was her domain and she was busy; a call about a young child with suspected meningitis had just come through and the ETA of the ambulance was five minutes.

"What's he doing on hospital premises?"

She knew, of course whom he meant and avoided Fronk's eye. He stood, down at heel and fiddled with both ear lobes as if plotting to escape through them.

"Mr Patel was brought in a few hours ago as an emergency having been found collapsed in the street."

"What's wrong with him?"

"Excessive alcohol consumption. He was virtually comatose."

Fronk was now nodding in agreement but said nothing; his admiration for Sister D. knew no bounds and if he had not had absolute certainty about the symmetrical size of her chest, he might have thought she was an Amazonian warrior.

"He can't stay here. He's been suspended; it's a serious breach of protocol." The Medical Director was at his most severe; cold, incontrovertible fact his proven weapon of choice.

"What about our duty of care? We wouldn't want anyone to accuse us of being negligent, would we?" Sister D. smiled saccharine deadly sweet. Fronk stopped fiddling with his ear lobes and hung onto them for safety as silence enfolded them like a shroud.

Graham Parsons, Director in name only, wordlessly conceded defeat and metaphorically fell at the feet of she who must be obeyed. However far be it from her to gloat; she merely acknowledged her undoubted superiority with a nod and agreed that she would indeed notify him as soon as the Suspended One had been discharged from the premises. No, it would not be necessary for him to be escorted by security at any stage, she would assume all responsibility for the accused while in the care of the Wyeminster Hospital. Her emphasis of accused was marked as a reminder of the principle of innocent before proven guilty. That man should be called Puritan not Parsons she mused as she proceeded down the corridor. Not that she particularly like Rohan Patel but she deeply resented any type of managerial interference in her department. How dare they? Any of them.

"I neither forgive nor forget, Fronk" she said. "And stop fiddling with your ears. It's unhygienic"

Whenever a child is rushed into an emergency department surrounded by paramedics and medical paraphernalia there is a frisson of fear amongst those in the waiting room. It would be a brave man or woman who would put themselves before the needs of a sick child – the reaction from everyone else alone would be enough to change their minds. People imagine their own being hurtled through the doors into the arms of the hospital staff and fall silent with concern and relief that it's someone else's child, not theirs. The boy on the trolley was small, only about five years old, pale and motionless. His skin was white and mottled red; his cheeks livid red, his eyes closed under dark-veined lids and ringed with darkness, giving him a hollow skull-like appearance accentuated by the sweat-wet hair that clasped his forehead and scalp. He had a drip in one arm which was being carried aloft by one of the paramedics; his mother followed immediately behind, speaking into a mobile in one hand, gripping a toy Thunderbird in the other.

"Meningitis" … she said as she followed the trolley "get here now …. No, I haven't done the glass test" she answered Mac as he grabbed one side of the trolley to help accelerate its progress and they disappeared into the acute treatment area.

"Glass test?" Shazza quizzed Dawn. "What's that?"

Dawn had absolutely no idea and was compelled, very reluctantly, to say so. No one else nearby knew either so there was no help for it but to resort to Tracy. All the proper medics had disappeared – like the police, never there when you need them Dawn lamented, before she turned her attention to the receptionist. She wouldn't know of course, Dawn confided to Shazza. They never do.

"You roll the glass over the rash. If it doesn't fade under the pressure it's a sign of meningitis" Tracy purred, pleased not for the child or the depth of her medical knowledge but because she had put one over on Dawn.

"He looked as if he had a rash" Shazza cooed with awe.

"Death is never far away" Dawn held forth in a subdued voice. "I should know. I've been that ill so many times. Stared death in the face I have."

"You never know what's around the corner" observed Shazza philosophically. "I don't mind waiting a bit longer if it's a kiddie though. It's only fair that kiddies go first."

"What will be will be. Only the good die young". Dawn shook her head sadly.

"I meant in the queue."

"Shut it!" Tracy shouted at them across the room. Surely somebody would take pity on her and treat those two cows so that they could go back to their coven or wherever they came from and leave her in peace.

"Miss Spanner? Could I have a word? It won't take long."

He looked as if someone had just died and it was his sad duty as the Medical Director, with Mr Kirmani, to tell her. But this was a hospital so maybe it was about staff cut backs? She'd heard the rumours which never actually either materialised or disappeared but hung around their lives like a bad smell. Well, she'd push them for all she could get, 'cos they always needed receptionists and it was a crap job anyway.

When Sonya Lewinski's allegation was put to her, it might have been better if someone had indeed passed away. Preferably her mother.

"But that's not what happened! He just left."

"Did he say anything to you?"

Tracy had stepped away from her work station and was concealed from the eyes in the waiting room but not their ears. Mr Kirmani was scrolling down her computer screen as if he knew what he was doing. Let him look – she had processed Andrez with his poxy 'z' by the letter and had nothing to hide. Or answer for, but that did not seem to be an option currently open to her.

"Not a word. He just upped and left. I didn't know he'd gone until he wasn't there. …This has nothing to do with me."

Dawn and Shazza knew better and exchanged 'she's got it coming' glances. Tracy's voice grew louder and now everyone could hear, even in the treatment area which became strangely quiet. Graham Parsons maintained an ever more modulated tone which drove the accused into a crescendo.

"I've done nothing wrong! I just check them in and out. No one treats me like this!"

Mr Kirmani returned and confirmed that yes, Mr Lewinski had been entered onto the system exactly as required in accordance with Tracy's assertions, which infuriated her even more. Of course he had; just like she said. Just like she did for everyone. And yes, she did remember him which was a frickin' miracle as there were so many people in A&E, especially on a Saturday night. He had been rude about her hair and then hadn't known where to sit so she'd helped him out. Even promised to let him know when he was called, in case he missed it.

Dawn's eyes opened wide to the point of craters at this definition of assistance and confirmed everything she already knew about the cheeky mare, who had had it coming for far too long.

"No one's blaming you" Mr Kirmani was saying a little too eagerly and then stopped as the Medical Director threw him the kind of look that said you can't make that kind of promise at this stage, not without a full investigation. The consultant chose to ignore him and continued. "We're just trying to find out what happened, Tracy."

"Here? And now?"

She had a point.

Perhaps they had underestimated her. Graham Parsons peered over his spectacles at the greasy hair and pale defiant face. You never can tell he reminded himself, and attempted to look less judgemental. She wasn't a union rep or anything like that, he had checked, but everyone these days was so informed and it wouldn't do to transgress the legal boundaries. Or alienate her was his afterthought, but he cared about the legalities more.

"You are absolutely right, of course."

Be conciliatory but don't smile. Let her think we're on her side. Time enough for what has to be done later…Monday. He glanced at his watch: tomorrow. "We'll discuss it at a more convenient time. …Tracy."

"So, you expect me just to go back to work now do you?"

How dare they? Either of them? She hated them both but not as much as Andrez and Sonya Lewinski. And Dawn and Shazza and everyone else sitting out in the waiting room and it was an outrage, an absolute effing outrage and it would serve them right if she walked out now and left them to it. See how they'd cope without her. But then it would look as if she had something to hide and she knew, so well, from all those years at home, the best way to survive. Show no emotion; endure. She rubbed her hands against her upper arms so that the scars shivered as she walked back to her computer screen and sat down, expressionless, suspended in time and place as the past collided with the present.

Mac held his breath and everyone else's as he prepared to press the glass over the child's stomach. The full length, from upper rib cage to pelvis. The Thunderbird's pyjama top had been removed and the elastic of the trousers eased down to clear a path. Just an ordinary tumbler from the canteen, kept in the treatment area alongside all the medical technology, had now become the arbiter of potential life and death. They had tested the child's arm in the same way but it was inconclusive so now it had to be the torso test.

So much noise yet absolute silence. They watched as he placed the cheap glass against the spotty, pale panting flesh.

"I'm looking to see if the rash fades when I press the glass against it" Mac said aloud, to no one in particular but knowing that they were all listening and that he held fate in his hand. "To see if the spots show up clearly through the glass."

"What if they do?" said the mother? Everyone else wished she hadn't.

"Let's see how we get on". He pushed the side of the cool glass into the hot little body, deflating the rising stomach, making a gentle depression like knuckles in kneaded dough.

"Thank Christ."

The dip in the belly had gone white, the spots had melted away, the silence faded and normal noise was heard again.

"It's a good sign" Mac said, "but we can't take any chances. Is he allergic to penicillin?... No? Good. 500 mg benzyl penicillin IV then 250 mg four times a day."

Someone nodded and moved away. He returned to the mother.

"Sometimes other viruses, less serious than meningitis, present with similar symptoms but your son'll have to be admitted to hospital immediately and kept under observation. We need to get his temperature down and keep a very close eye on him. Sister?"

What he and she knew, and the mother did not, was that there was almost certainly no bed for the child in the Wyeminster. Mac also realised that he had erred – he had used the first-person plural when it should have been the third person – 'his temperature needs to be brought down' was what he should have said. Not necessarily by us, you understand, but by someone, probably somewhere else. That's what he should have implied and now they would have to go through the chaos of transferring a sick child to another more specialised centre miles away, by ambulance (if they could find one.) Or they could keep him on a trolley somewhere – at least that made observation easy – until a bed became available.

Sister D. threw him a look of weary disdain and put on her it's most regrettable but all for the best face as she turned to the mother, who would probably react in one of two ways. She would either simply accept and follow or she would go ballistic. Anxiety did that to people. Fortunately, she acquiesced although the boy's father on the end of her phone was more belligerent. Only when she told him to piss off back to his sorry second life did it become evident that she was a single parent. Sister D. immediately offered tea (made by someone else).

Tracy was texting, furiously, cursing predictive text not quite under her breath so that Dawn and Shazza could take a lively interest. Her brief disappearance at the hands of the scruffy old chap who was 'clearly more than he seemed tho' you could never tell by appearances could you?" was intriguing. They were desperate. It was impossible not to want to know.

"Fired?"

"Warning at least."

"Who's she texting?"

"Lawyer?"

"Nah. People like her don't have lawyers. That's just on the telly."

"Union rep maybe?"

"Yeah. Almost certain. She won't get an answer at this time of night though, silly cow."

Tracy was in fact texting both and neither in the form of her half-sister, whom she hated only marginally less than her mother and her step father but who did at least have some merit in that she was employed as a legal secretary in a solicitor's office. Tracy had a five-year head start on Stacey but little else. Shorter, wider, spottier (at least she had had more acne) and darker haired than her younger sibling, Tracy was also less academic, less popular (especially with her mother) less articulate and undeniably less attractive. She even had less Nectar points. She had never two-timed a boy, received a Valentine's Day card from anyone other than herself or been whistled at in the street – not that she approved of such sexist behaviour but it would have been nice to able to complain about such insults. Stacey did, all the time. Now Stacey, who had an only twice-divorced golf playing husband who had a time share in Florida which he never used it, worked in a local legal firm and knew everything about The Law. No one made up bundles better than she did – the judge had said so – the solicitors would be lost without her; was there anything she did not know? they would marvel as they sought her advice. Even if half of what Stacey said was bullshit, she was obviously working in the right place with the right people so it was to her, at this ungodly hour, that Tracy turned. Plus, there was no one else. Of course, there wouldn't be a response at this time of night; Stacey would be out. She liked a drink – nothing cheap, mind – so would be well hungover until she started again on Sunday but at least Tracy knew that her message would have been sent. Nothing much would happen before Monday anyway.

Chapter Ten

She did not see the man standing at the desk; had no concept of his existence until he made a hesitant apology for being there. So sorry to interrupt, especially when she was busy but he thought he ought to come in. After what they had been saying on the news.

"Yeah?"

Tracy did not watch the news, did not much care. Problems enough of her own. I mean, she knew about climate change and all that – well, you couldn't miss it could you? It never stopped frickin' raining but she had her doubts about global warming: the summers were always crap, especially on her days off. She liked *Hello* magazine though.

"I think I might have a temperature."

Tracy sighed.

"Taken anything for it?"

"Paracetamol. Like they said."

Tracy put her mobile to one side and looked up. Just another client, as her line manager liked to call them. Tosser.

"Any other symptoms?"

"Runny nose and a bit of a cough. Sort of achy but nothing else."

"Had a flu jab?"

"No." The accused hung his head in shame and admitted his guilt. Then remorse. He really was very sorry: knew should have made the time and effort. All his own fault, and all that advertising about it!

"Yeah."

She sighed again. Another time waster, on her watch, at…she checked the time on her screen … two bloody a.m.

At that moment the double doors hurtled into action. After the exodus of the not-so-ills and the passage of time into the early hours of the day of rest they had been taking things easier. Well-earned respite they had both agreed and closed themselves with relief, reposing shoulder to shoulder in the hope of mutual slumber.

A young man, probably in his early teens, was to be seen smearing himself against the reinforced glass of one of the doors – the one on the right, which was deeply shocked. Just as he was nodding off! Oh well, it went with the job he supposed and moved aside. Then was appalled. There was blood on his glass, plastered all over it where the young man was slumped, one hand pressed against his chest and the other slapped against the door which moved as quickly as it could to get away from the mess. As the doors parted the man fell into the waiting room, slippery with blood.

Tracy saw and shouted for a crash team even as she was lifting the hospital phone to summon help. Dawn and Shazza saw and screamed as they gasped and gaped. Everyone else watched and gawped. Even Thumb Man was taken aback by the amount of blood. The queue for the toilet turned as an eel to see and the toilet door opened even as the incumbent was pulling up his trousers to see what the fuss was about.

"Crash team. Emergency department reception. Now. We've got a stabbing."

From the treatment area appeared a cohort of medics led by Mac and Fronk, running. Sister D. was close behind, not running, but surprisingly agile for one of her bulk. Dawn was impressed in spite of herself. Shazza was engrossed. Mr Kirmani arrived, slightly sweaty, rolling up his sleeves with latex covered hands.

"Chest" Mac shouted.

"In the chest" Tracy said into the phone.

"Right in the heart!" Dawn pronounced with awe. Shazza clutched at her own.

"Semi-conscious with heavy bleeding" Mac was saying as he bent over the young man who by now was discolouring the floor. Then the crash team were there and surrounded them both. Mac was seen to stand aside and the others closed ranks about the victim who was moved, turned, lifted and transported onto a trolley, smothered in medical equipment and helping hands.

"Resus" Mr Kirmani ordered and the cluster began rapidly shifting.

"Can't see a bloody thing" Dawn complained, twisting as much as she could without raising a buttock from her seat.

"Police." Tracy was making a second call. "Wyeminster Hospital. Emergency Department. … An incident. … Course I frickin' am, I'm the receptionist. It's a stabbing…No, not here, just the victim… well he's bleeding out all over the waiting room so yeah, it is serious. … Morons" she added as she slammed down the phone. The man without the flu vaccination was still standing at the reception desk. Tracy screeched.

"You'll have to wait. Sit down or something but keep out of the way. I'll deal with you in a minute. Can't you see this is serious?" she added in exasperation. Was he a complete idiot?

The stabbed man disappeared leaving only the echo of shouted instructions and a slimy red pool to show where he had lain. That and the bloody hand print on the glass of the door which was shuddering with horror and had almost come to a halt. But not quite. Mr Kirmani's voice could be heard from the land of the treated

"And onto the bed … one, two, three, lift. We need bloods for cross match, U plus Es and FBC, clotting…asap. Mac, cannula in? BP?"

"Low but holding. Systolic 70."

"We've got to stop the bleeding" the consultant was saying. "We're losing everything we're putting in. Get onto the blood bank."

No one in the waiting room heard the entrance doors open but every single person there could not miss what happened next.

Just as Tracy was girding herself to summon Kolya and his cleaning trolley – damn it, he would still be on duty – there was a tooth enamel tingling scream. It was Dawn. Boy, could that fat lady sing. The noise was so acidic, so sharp, so loud that for a moment there was nothing else, then began a cacophonous chorus of shouts, gasps, less sustained screams and moving furniture. Standing in the doorway, framed, like a Mongol invader, stood a man with a knife. Not just any man, but one with straggly hair to his shoulders under some sort of close-fitting hat, a long shirt beneath a padded vest, thick socks, army boots and very little else except a back pack. His legs were bare. He carried an exceptionally sharp kitchen knife covered in blood in one hand and in his face, he wore murder. Nor did he stand there long, but almost instantly sprang into the room, tense-buttocked and sinewy-thighed like a well- endowed mountain goat. As instructed, he made straight for the most prominent person in the room: Dawn. She was certainly the largest. Unable to move she suddenly found herself gripped manfully around the neck by a bare, hairy arm with a knife pressed against her third chin, in pursuit of her throat. A little more pressure and it would find that precious channel which was taut with fear and the exertion of screaming.

"Shut up, bitch" the knifeman hissed at her. Dawn stopped so fast that her throat almost went into spasm and she had to gulp, which was terrifying because it brought her into even closer proximity with the sticky blade.

"Everyone get back" the man with the knife ordered and there was an immediate exodus of people, chairs, bags, coats, comestibles and beverages to the far recesses of the room, far away from the toilet from which the queue had miraculously disappeared. Only Tracy was left cowering behind her desk; even the man who thought he might have a temperature had joined the throng on the other side of the room *en route* to the corridor beyond and safety. If only they could get further into the hospital premises; anything to escape. Shazza led the party; she had only just met Dawn, after all, and life was precious. Dawn was a big girl and could look after herself. She would have to. Behind her the man seemed slight and insignificant, dwarfed, but then he was the one with the knife which undoubtably gave him an advantage. If Shazza felt guilty about abandoning ship this was outweighed by fear. She knew from experience with a badly opened baked bean can that sharp metal cut through flesh – any amount of it – like hot ghee and no number of chins would save the helpless hostage. It was all so unfortunate she thought as she headed in the opposite direction.

Almost concealed by the bulk in front him, the knifeman had to shout to be heard but managed to twist himself slightly to one side of his victim so that he could monitor what was happening. What he saw was most gratifying. Such terror on all their faces! What they had said was true. It was his vocation; he had to save them. The evil that was Dawn had to be eliminated and it was so easy when you had Right in one hand and a knife in the other.

"Mother of Satan" he hissed again, loudly enough for Dawn and the voices to hear. "They told me you'd be here."

Dawn inhaled so deeply with fear that the man was almost displaced and had to bend to accommodate the sudden expansion of her chest, but he was nothing if not tenacious and the knife never moved.

"Don't move, you whore" he whispered to her then "Or she gets it" he shouted for the benefit of his audience. "She's got it coming" he added earnestly.

Tracy would have liked to agree but safety came first; she had her hand pressed hard against the panic button below the desk, increasing the pressure as much as the already depressed button would allow. Where the hell was help when you needed it? WTF, she'd already called the police for an urgent incident and they still hadn't arrived. Visions of every terrorist movie she had ever seen flickered through her brain as she pressed the button ever harder and reached for the phone.

"He's wearing a dress thing with a stab vest and something on his back. I think it's a suicide bomber" she told the person at the other end. "Please. Help."

In acute treatment they could hear the commotion, the alarm going off, see the red light maniacally flashing and yet do nothing. The patient who had been stabbed was critically ill; he was bleeding prolifically, over them all. It was even dripping off the bed onto the floor where it splashed merrily into an ever-increasing puddle. The man's shirt had been ripped apart from the point where it had been sliced by the knife blade and now lay spread alongside his chest like a badly opened butter wrapper. The consultant was panting as he thumped and pressed the blood-spattered mess below his hands. Manual CPR was clearly not going to work.

They did not even know his name.

"Adrenaline 1 milligram. Charge the defibrillator."

A high-pitched whine, like the wail of a disorientated banshee filled the air and clashed with the shrieking alarm that was still being firmly pressed by a desperate Tracy. The beep of the monitor booting up punctuated the uproar.

"Fluids stat. Start massive transfusion protocol. O negative; tranexamic acid. … Ready to shock? … Stand clear everyone."

There was a hearty thwack as the electric charge made contact with flesh. Then silence. They all counted the seconds in their heads … "one…two…" and waited for the monitor to take up the count.

Nothing.

"And again. Stand clear."

Another thwack, another silence, another two seconds and then, miraculously, the monitor came to life, beating with an orderly rhythm strangely at odds with the pandemonium around it. A communal sigh of relief ensued - which was short lived.

"We'll never stop the haemorrhage unless we can get into the whole chest cavity."

Mr Kirmani's latex gloves could barely contain the passage of blood snaking up his arms towards the barrier of his rolled-up shirt sleeves.

"We've got to do direct heart massage and repair the damage or we'll lose him. It'll have to be a clamshell thoracotomy. There's no time for anything else."

"A clamshell thoracotomy? In Resus?" Mac was incredulous. Crack the chest? Here? Now? This never happened, not at Wyeminster. Mac had only ever seen it done on You Tube; it was a once in a lifetime moment and he was there to share it! Wow!

Less thrilling but equally time sensitive were the events outside in the waiting area. Just as the decision was being made to open the victim's chest to affect a rescue, the double doors let go of all caution and flung themselves wide apart. In poured a pack of bulky black figures in protective helmets, stab vests, heavy booted and even more heavily armed. An elite anti-terrorist squad had arrived. No one in Wyeminster had the least idea that such a squad existed, although it was known that the headquarters of the SAS was discreetly located in the area. Even the police themselves, who had been ordered to hold back until the area had been made safe, were awed and honoured. A stabbing was one thing, but a suicide bomber! Outside London or Manchester! On their patch. Think of the publicity!

Peering uncomfortably around the bulk of his hostage, the knifeman had a clear view of the doors and saw the enemy approach, but was not afraid. They had told him to expect this; it was all part of the conspiracy and he knew what he had to do. Mentally it had been rehearsed over and over, in and out of sleep, and he was ready. Dawn however, was not. As she felt the blade scrape against her trachea, she thought she would faint. Not only was she to have her windpipe severed but now she was to be shot to death. And she had only come in for a bad back. It was Shazza who had the sore throat – why couldn't it have been her who had been taken hostage?

Speaking of her bad back, the knifeman was pulling her away from the encroaching gunmen and it really hurt. She wanted to say something but did not dare. She was being edged backwards, in the direction of the reception desk, only Tracy was no longer there. The knifeman was sweating with the effort. Why had he chosen someone so big? They had told him to take the most prominent person in the room but only now did it occur to him that maybe prominent and large were not necessarily the same thing. Too late now though, and at least she would provide plentiful cover if there was any shooting. Such were his thoughts as he hauled his fleshy shield towards the wall behind him in the direction of a door designated Strictly No Admittance, from whence he would stage his final showdown and/or make a strategic withdrawal via the forbidden exit. It would take him further into the hospital, admittedly, but he had already decided against taking this hostage with him. Far too slow. Dawn shuffled her hefty legs and swollen feet as fast as she could as they retreated and for the first time in her life wondered if she was in some way to blame. Then maybe this would not have happened.

Graham Parsons had no such qualms, but for the first time in his life he too was experiencing a new emotion – confusion. Everything suddenly seemed to have changed, all the rules were breaking and the boundaries had shifted to vanishing point. A man was about to be split open in the Resus area, not even in theatre, by medics not even scrubbed up; the panic alarm bell was hammering in his ears, lights were flashing all over the place, the squeal of the defibrillator still resonated and he could hear the shouting on the other side of the wall in the waiting area. It sounded like an army exercise on Salisbury Plain and he did not know where to go, in which direction to turn, who to address or what to do. The child with the virus that they had thought might be meningitis was crying, his mother was desperately trying to comfort him, there was a nurse with artificial holes in his ears and an alleged sexual predator drunk in a cubicle with his genitalia hanging out. And as if that was not enough, he had been accosted by a middle-aged Barbie doll who wanted to know where her daughter's butt cheek had gone because it was private property and she wanted to send it back to Turkey for a refund.

New to him too was the impossibility of being able to systematically prioritise his actions: everything seemed to have to be done at once. Who was to say what was more important than the other? There was a distinct possibility of sudden death on either side of the wall beside which he was standing and he did not know where he should be. Kirmani seemed pretty in control, medically speaking, and the noise in the waiting room had subsided – a military voice was shouting orders and manoeuvres seemed to have come to a halt. As he removed his glasses to wipe the lenses, as if this would supply him with a solution to his indecision, he heard sturdy approaching footsteps and glanced up. It was Tracy.

Having set off every panic button, alarm and light that she could find, Tracy had made the informed decision to get the hell out of reception and find safety. She had slipped away from her desk – left the computer running which was strictly against security rules but WTF? It would put itself to sleep eventually and she wasn't risking her life to shut it down. Her line manager would just have to suck it up. Anyway, who was going to sneak a look at the information on the screen in the middle of a full-scale terrorist attack?

In the Resus area Mr Kirmani was preparing the clam thoracotomy and Mac, to his great joy, was to assist. Although they had not yet confirmed his name, the patient had been identified as a young male, about 17 or 18. Even now one of the nurses was going through the iPhone found lodged tightly in the back pocket of his knock off designer jeans. They knew he was an avid Tweeter, Snapchatterer and Instagrammer, but apparently, he used a pseudonym – surely no one could really be called Wakizashi2003? Whatever he was called, he had no idea what was about to happen.

"Keep him supine and as still as you can but keep the CPR going. Intubated?" he asked the anaesthetist who nodded as he somehow bagged the body despite the bumping and pressing of the cardiac massage. I know it's not ideal in terms of preparation but we've no choice… Right. Ready? … I'm going in…" here he deftly inserted the scalpel blade which sank into the flesh below the left nipple without a murmur "at the fifth intercostal space mid axillary line … all the way down to his shoulder blade then I'm joining the two cuts…" By which time he had removed the blade and was slicing in on the other side.

"Scissors!"

He punched through the intercostal muscles, blunt and rough and brutal, the yellow fringed edges of the wound flapping with the movement of the CPR while the scissors probed and pushed, smashing inwards deeper and wider to make a path for the bone cutter to come in and divide the sternum between the two cuts.

"Clamp!"

Metal teeth fixed open the chest as his hands disappeared within in pursuit of the heart.

"We may need to clamp the aorta.... the big clamp ... we need more blood. Don't clamp the oesophagus". For a split second he stopped, to evaluate. "I can feel a pulse.... Okay. Cardiac massage...." Mac's hands had pulled away to allow Mr Kirmani's to pump and press within the man's torso, kneading the heart like gory pastry into shape and life.

It worked. The monitor picked up the thread and beeped back into action.

Not even time for a brief moment of self-congratulation.

"Okay, let's find the hole in the heart and put a big stitch in it to stop the bleeding. Then we can get him into theatre where he'll be closed up when he's stable. It's a bit of a mess but at least he's back with us."

Graham Parsons would have liked to help, but did not know how. Thus it was he found himself in the corridor, face to face with Tracy.

"Miss Spanner. Are you alright?"

She was, not that he cared, and she would have been a great deal better if she had not bumped into him, she thought, immediately planning her escape. The last thing she needed just now was more accusations and allegations from a reptile such as Graham effing Parsons. She eyed him suspiciously then swivelled her glance to the wall beside him. The emergency exit! Yes, all she had to do was approach and deflect, open the door and let herself out. There was so much going on in the waiting area that no one would notice her. She found herself experiencing unexpected appreciation and gratitude to Dawn for being so large and immobile that the knifeman would not have been able to move very far from his original position. She would also absorb much of the blast from any explosion. Brutal, but true Tracy admitted mentally as she twisted out of the way of the Medical Director who was replacing his spectacles, and heaved the bar of the emergency door downward as she forced it open.

On the other side of the door the man with the backpack was caught completely by surprise. Had the armed men come in the back way as well? He hadn't thought of that. He felt the heavy door hammer into his back with astonishment and then pain, which bounced up his spine into his arms which flew outwards like a bird launching into flight. The knife against Dawn's throat was suddenly up, away, airborne, out of his grasp, sliding through the air as a skate on ice. He watched it go. They all watched it go … soar … glide…. then descend, without so much as a shiver. It landed clumsily on the grubby floor and slid to an ungainly halt, impeded by its stickiness, dust and a chipped skirting board. At once a large black boot stamped itself upon the offensive weapon that seemed to wither and shrink out of all significance.

Dawn only realised that she was no longer in imminent danger of having her throat cut when the man behind her gasped – winded with the impact of the opening door as well as blind-sided by surprise. While no match for Dawn in either height or width, Tracy was by no means an insubstantial mass and her full weight against the emergency door was too much for the slight frame of the attacker. He found himself impounded in the soft back of his hostage, fighting for breath and self-control. Escape was impossible; suffocation more than likely. It was almost a relief to find himself roughly extracted from his fleshy confinement by gloved hands and strong arms. Even the cold steel of the armed weapons against his head and the way his hands were angrily twisted together and tied behind his back as he was laid out on the floor was somehow preferable. As he lay, alone, surrounded, uncomfortable and bony with his nose pressed against the hard floor which smelt of disinfected vomit and urine, he offered no resistance. They had told him this might happen. It was all part of the plan.

"Suspect is disarmed and on the ground. Repeat. Disarmed and on the ground. No sign of explosive devices or incendiaries – it seems to be a backpack and it's definitely not a suicide vest. In fact…" the voice hesitated, "it looks like a gilet – one of those padded sleeveless jobs you get in Millets or those outdoor pursuit shops."

The voice was loud and unanswered – talking into a phone or something. It continued.

"No, not armed. Not really dressed either…. It's a beanie hat. … No trousers or underpants, just a long shirt, socks and walking boots. …Yes, it's a stand down."

Tracy of course, was the heroine of the hour. She had single-handedly, albeit inadvertently, disarmed a knife-wielding intruder, saved the hospital from an unprecedented suspected terrorist attack and, most unexpected of all, rescued Dawn from a ghastly, murderous death. Even Tracy was surprised, but not half as astonished as Dawn. It was an emotional moment. Both women had been placed on chairs, side by side, by the armed rescuers and neither knew what to say to the other, Dawn because she was in a state of shock and Tracy because she still did not realise quite what had happened. However, the spontaneous applause that erupted from the spectators, prompted by Shazza, was most gratifying. Really, Dawn was thinking, this has been quite an eventful evening and it wasn't over yet! Everyone was being so attentive; the nurse with hollow ears (shame he was male but not his fault) had taken her blood pressure and offered assistance in case she felt dizzy or faint. She didn't but a cup of hot sweet tea and something to eat would help – it had been such an ordeal. She would never get over it. Yes, of course they would see to her bad back, as soon as they could. Did she need pain relief in the meantime? No? How brave she was! The Press would be here, wouldn't they? She managed to turn her head towards the double doors in case they had already arrived and wondered which was her best side.

Chapter Eleven

Graham Parsons was fulsome in his praise. Tracy was marvellous, an asset to the hospital, such a team player; on behalf of everyone he wanted to express his thanks and appreciation for her bravery. Really, quite remarkable.

Tracy did not believe a word of it. However, she accepted the cup of coffee – no, no sugar – she was fine and quite sweet enough, thank you and was not in the least bit shocked. Made of sterner stuff. Yes, she could go back to her position at reception. Besides, there was no one else, was there? So it was that she found herself once more *in situ* behind her (still running) computer screen, peering out at the not-quite returned to normal waiting room. The knifeman had been vigorously removed by the armed heavies, his knife and backpack had been bagged as evidence and now only the police and a couple of anti-terrorists remained. It had been ascertained that the knifeman had been working alone (in spite of the voices he said he heard) and the hospital had now been declared safe. Statements were being taken from the multitude of witnesses, all keen to have their say, rehearsing for the Press who had been seen prowling outside.

The hospital was still on a security lockdown which meant no new admissions through the door, at least for the time being. Excellent news for Graham Parsons who could now anticipate the restoration of acceptable Government target waiting times. God moved in mysterious ways indeed.

Dawn could not stop talking. Pity the poor police officer tasked with recording all that, Tracy thought. He would soon be in the one in need of medical treatment. As for her, well, heroism was its own reward so her statement had been short, pithy and modest. She had been aware of the Medical Director's approbation as she spoke and just as he looked forward to meeting Government guidelines, she assumed that all that nasty business concerning the Lewinskis would now be treated with the derision it deserved. What a shame she had panicked and contacted Stacey. But that cow – such a minger – would never reply, so no harm done.

The man who had neglected to have the flu jab was on the other side of the room, just about to sit down after being interviewed by the police. Tracy waved him over to the reception area.

"Right" she said. "Where were we? ... Are you okay?"

He did not look well.

"A bit hot" he said, sweating. "It's warm in here."

"Not really. You might be running a temperature – should've had that flu jab. I'll take some details then someone will take a look at you."

His name was Alex Chown, he was 34, lived in Wyeminster and had recently come back from holiday. That was nice, Tracy said.

"Somewhere hot?"

"China."

"Big place. Whereabouts?"

"Wuhan."

"Never heard of it".

"I don't feel well."

She looked at him more closely. He did look a bit peaky – pale, moist and rheumy eyed. He gave a scratchy cough which seemed to shake his body from the inside out and made him stagger to regain his balance.

"Take a seat and the triage nurse will be out in a minute." She reached for the phone to summon Fronk.

"Some bloke with a fever who says he's been abroad" she said into the receiver.

"Whereabouts?"

"China."

"Shit."

Seconds later Fronk appeared, ear lobes swinging as he cantered over to the man at the reception desk.

"China?" Fronk asked him.

"Yeah" he replied, and coughed again.

"Not Wuhan?" Fronk pleaded.

"How'd you know that?" Tracy enquired, impressed.

The man wiped his wet forehead. "I don't feel well" he said, and collapsed onto the floor.

Now Graham Parsons could help. This was exactly what he was made to do as the Wyeminster Hospital Trust Medical Director. It was all about systems, protocols, and organisation – exactly what he excelled at. He would be a pragmatic, calm, informed and magnificent…show them how it should be done. Already he was assimilating the situation and drawing up contingency plans. He sat in his office – thank goodness the lights had not been turned off; he could get straight to work – and briefed the Trust's Chief Executive over the phone. It would be better if she came in, yes, but therein lay a problem. The hospital was on an immediate infectious disease lockdown for a suspected case of COVID 19. Coronavirus. No one could come in or go out without screening, full Hazmat protective apparel and further screening on departure… with possible precautionary self-isolation afterwards. All those exposed to possible infection, including himself, would have to be quarantined. Yes, it was a blessing in a way that he had been on the premises. Now there would a central co-ordinator in place to command and monitor the situation. It was a notifiable disease and yes, of course the appropriate National Health authorities had already been informed. All those in wards and areas of the hospital safe from possible infection would have to be discharged or evacuated to other hospitals, hopefully not too far away. Those in quarantine would have to be tested and accommodated on the premises. Unfortunately, due to an unprecedented sequence of events in the hospital that night, there were serious ramifications beyond the hospital itself.

He went on to explain about the suspected terrorist attack which, regrettably, meant that the virus was already outside the hospital and that all those involved in the incident, yes, including the elite anti-terrorist squad, would have to be isolated and tested. At least there were police on the premises…that might ease potential organisational issues…. He did mean riots and yes, obviously it was not ideal but he was more than capable of dealing with it, in every detail and was already very much in control. … Why had the suspected case not been immediately identified and isolated, preventing so much exposure to infection?

It was a good question and he had the answer. The fault lay, fairly and squarely, with the Emergency Department receptionist, who had failed to process the suspected case in a timely manner so the sick patient – yes, displaying symptoms of the virus - had been forced to sit and wait, thereby creating a much greater risk of infection. In Miss Spanner's defence (that was the name of the receptionist, yes) there had been a great deal going on so one could argue mitigating circumstances, but the fault was essentially hers. If the man had been heard and processed as required by the excellent guidelines laid down by The Trust, he would have been instantly diagnosed and isolated. The scale of the problem which, he had to admit, was much larger than he would have wanted, was entirely down to the incompetence of the receptionist.

Having thrown Tracy under the bus, run her over and metaphorically reversed back to complete the job, it did little to alleviate her injuries to inform the incandescent Chairman that it had been Tracy who had disarmed the knifeman. After all, it had happened accidentally, so she could not really take the credit, could she? It had been a lucky accident – could have been anyone who just happened to open the door at that particular moment – and the real work of making the area safe had been carried out by the armed squad; the police had been marvellous. Team work; essential services working hand in hand to maintain public safety and confidence. Yes, they could certainly emphasise that aspect of events with The Press who were even now sniffing around the hospital, invading the lines of communication, hi-jacking the premises and making a thorough nuisance of themselves. It would be a pleasure to impose a restriction zone. As much to keep the hounds out as the afflicted infected in. He was tempted to smile when he said this but refrained – not on The Sabbath. The Wyeminster Hospital was, at once, to be became a designated infection and quarantine Coronavirus centre and he was to be its leader. Public Health England had already made the momentous decision, everyone was talking about it and his own name was being bandied about by Those Who Mattered, even to the top rung at No 10. No one seemed to mind that he was a rheumatologist now.

Things were not going well. On many levels. A team of staff had been selected and summoned in addition to those already on the premises who would be required to run the hospital. Those in-patients safe from any possibility of contagion were being culled, in the nicest possible way, either in the form of summary discharging via rear entrances or prepared for evacuation to other medical facilities. AT least it had stopped raining. The early hours of Sunday morning did not make for ideal timing for such arrangements; response was slow and reluctant. No one seemed to want them – now or later.

"No beds", "no room", "over-subscribed", "full", "trolleys in the corridor", and "are you insane?" were among the more polite responses from the Wyeminster's erstwhile medical neighbours, even as far away as the East Midlands and the English Riviera. In the end, threats and ultimatums had to be used, Medical Director to Medical Director and the unwanted infirm were shovelled as quickly as possible, drips, medical notes and all, into hastily assembled modes of transport – anything to get them off the premises. So, while the front of the hospital, designed to accommodate multitudes and their cars remained strangely quiet and barren, the back of the hospital was a seething broth of noise, ignored instructions, complaints, moans, groans, squeaky trolley wheels, feet slopping through puddles, slamming doors and motor engines. Even the Press had abandoned the main entrance and were holding an artificially-lit vigil alongside the exodus which was illuminated with flash photography like fireworks. The double doors leading to the waiting room were bereft – ignored and unappreciated. No one now crossed their consecrated threshold; they descended into a dark depression and clung to each other for comfort as they gazed mournfully out onto the deserted concourse.

Inside the waiting room things were little better.

"What d'you mean we've gotta stay here?" Dawn led the revolt, from the front. Nothing like a new drama to dissipate the trauma of another and, God, hadn't she had enough of it for one evening? This was getting ridiculous.

"I just need something for my back and then I'm going home. No knifemen there" she said to Shazza loudly enough for everyone to hear. "It's a disgrace, that's what it is. I'm in a terrible state. I only came in for medication, If I'd known what was going to happen, I'd have stayed at home…We all would…wouldn't we?"

Yes, of course they would. Insurrection was in the air, mostly in the direction of Tracy. If she'd got the infected man out of the way when she should have, then none of this would have happened, would it? It was all her fault. Now they would be stuck in this dump for… what… you're joking? … Two weeks? Fourteen days? No way!

"Of course it applies to them all. Everyone who has come into contact with the suspected Coronavirus patient must be stripped and showered before being issued with protective clothing. Staff need to be cleansed and screened first then dressed in complete Hazmat gear before attending to those exposed to possible infection. It needs to be done in an orderly way. There is no place for panic or fuss."

Graham Parsons was sitting at his desk, Clear, direct information and instructions, just like those he was dispensing now, were all that was required for an orderly implementation of the necessary – absolutely essential – procedures that must be followed. It was not difficult and he refused to believe that any sensible person would refuse to comply. Clearly, he had not met Dawn. He was speaking to Mr Kirmani who was sending despatches from the battle field. Alex Chown, referred to now as The Contagious One, had been placed, alone, inside a plastic tent within a small side room as far away from human contact as physically possible. He lay, sedated, feverish, achy and wheezy while Mr Kirmani watched, accompanied by Fronk and Sister D. All three were clad in white, like incipient larvae, lumpy, shapeless and scrunched, their faces blurred behind perspex and their bodies shrouded in ill-fitting Hazmat suits. Nothing could get in; nothing to get out. They were as isolated in their way as the patient in the tent. Only height and width gave an indication as to identity. Sister D was the very rotund to the point of square larva with stretched buttocks, Mr Kirmani the tallest and Fronk the slightest. Without any distinguishing ear discs, he just seemed small: invisible. They were all troops now; Hazmat suits made them all the same. Seniority, status, leather soled shoes, uniforms, body art no matter how accomplished, were all concealed from view and they were amorphous in the face of the enemy. "The Challenge" as their great leader the Medical Director chose to call it and they were all united once more by corporate eye rolling.

No, Mr Kirmani did not know when the test results would be back; yes, of course the blood samples had been sent off straight away but in the absence of an all-night laboratory in the Wyeminster necessitating the transport of The Contagious One's phials to a centre of excellence some fifty odd miles away, it would be some time. They were considering a CT test to establish if there were any obstacles in TCO's lungs which would explain his respiratory problems, a sure sign of Coronavirus. About which, he had to admit, they knew very little. But they were learning. Fast. Of course, he agreed with the Medical Director. Everything possible should be done immediately to contain the suspected infection but did the Medical Director agree that this was not going to be easy? Especially as they had managed to ascertain that their carrier had returned with his family from Wuhan ten days ago and had been living a normal life in Wyeminster and its environs since then? It was beginning to look as if the whole of Wyeminster would be declared a red zone and be locked down with the knifeman.

The police confined to the premises stared dismally out of the double doors at their liberated colleagues on the other side of the blue and white incident tape in the land of the free. Two weeks in this place, with this motley crew. Already they had earmarked potential troublemakers and insurrectionists; Dawn posed the biggest threat, in every sense of the word. They did not like the look of the porter either, the one with the axe murderer face. He had been summoned to clean the gory stains on one of the main doors and they could almost hear the screams of pain of the glass as the man scraped and chafed at the dried-on blood, without uttering a word. The receptionist had identified him only as Kolya, as if that was enough.

The receptionist. She seemed like a nice lass – or woman, it was hard to tell. That hair could have belonged to anyone over the age of 15 and she was shapeless enough to make physical assessment almost impossible. Not fit though, and a face like an unmade bed, crumpled rather than creased except around the mouth which was fixed in a kind of twist. Over plucked eyebrows put her into the not-so contemporary bracket though; all the younger women these days had heavy statement brows that were pencilled in if the hair was lacking, and sometimes even if it wasn't. How could she not have identified a possible Coronavirus carrier? Even the police, upholders of justice, law and order, were tempted to lynch her. This was all her fault. Therefore, they continued to stare morosely out of the doors while their families, lives and loved ones were put on hold for the next fortnight.

With the help of social media and a long telephone call, it had been established that Alex Chown, TCO, had indeed been living and working in Wyeminster since his return from Coronavirus Central in China and had thus, potentially, infected the whole town. His wife and children had accompanied him – it was a family holiday after all - and were even now being visited by medics and Public Health England desperate to track their movements and contacts over the last ten days. Schools, the High Street, the twenty-four/seven supermarket so favoured by Billy even if he did not have his mobility scooter, the Gate of the Heavens restaurant which was their family business, the local leisure centre (weekly swimming and Tae Kwando lessons for both children), the cash and carry in the nearby city, wherever they had walked their dog (could dogs catch it? Mrs Chown was very anxious about that), the Three Barrels pub where Alex liked a pint and was a member of the darts team (doing well in the league thanks to a win last Saturday): the list went on and on and the number of possible victims grew longer and longer.

"What do you mean we don't have any mobile military showers? We must have." Graham Parsons was not in the mood for incompetence. "They must all be showered as soon as possible, as part of the deep clean process. Time is of the essence." Some legalese will concentrate your mind he thought, as he awaited the response from the other end of the phone. Alas, it made no difference. The Trust HR manager had been in touch with Admin who had contacted Stores, NHS Supply Chain, the off-site laundry, the kitchens, even the pharmacy and there was not a single mobile shower of any description to be had. Perhaps they could order some, but from whom? Amazon? And all of this in the early hours of Sunday morning. It had been extremely difficult even to contact these people but the HR manager had pulled out all the stops and achieved the impossible. However, she was pleased to note that at the first mention of Coronavirus, she had had their undivided attention. She really was doing all she could….

It was not enough.

They needed them now. Yes, the army might be able to help but that would take time. That they did not have. Had the HR manager not heard him? He, Mr Graham Parsons, the Medical Director working closely with the Wyeminster Trust Chairman and Public Health England was in urgent need of facilities with which to body-wash a waiting room full of people plus medical staff, support staff, admin staff, police, those in the treatment room and at least one member of senior management i.e. himself.

"Staff changing rooms? … Yes, I suppose that could work…. Not ideal, but possible."

Then, of course, there was the issue of sterile replacement clothing, face masks, protective gear, food, sleeping arrangements. Having the fact that they were hospital so wasn't this par for the course pointed out to him by his disgruntled colleague, still in her pyjamas, did not enhance the Medical Director's perspective, no matter how intently he peered over his glasses.

Tracy was given the dubious honour of announcing the verdict to those in the waiting room – all still there, penned-in like livestock but far less amenable. The digital notice board on the wall had now been updated. Predicted waiting times had been abandoned (fourteen days would not be well received) and instead it delivered the message about showers with a kind of lop-sided grin. Mocking – see how it feels to be thrown into disarray it seemed to gloat as its words toiled uphill.

"Whaddya mean we have to take all our clothes off and take a shower?" Dawn led the protest. Upright. Outraged. Indignation had brought her to her feet. Unfortunately her objection was not as fully endorsed as she would have liked; the drunks, now awake and relatively alert were more than happy to oblige, especially as there was a tidy amount of totty amongst their number. Were the staff changing rooms mixed sex? was their only real concern.

Tracy was reaching her limit. Having descended so rapidly from the heroine of the hour to public enemy number one, when none of this was her fault - how the hell was she supposed to process patients when a terrorist was rampaging through her waiting room? – she burned. Perhaps they would like to have a go? If they thought they could do a better job? They were welcome to try. Her fibromyalgia was playing up, she ached everywhere, her head was pounding and another IBS attack was inevitable. She could already feel her colon throwing a tantrum.

"No, they're not frickin' mixed. This isn't a sauna… men to the right, women to the left. Police escort. Might as well make yourselves useful." She barked, bared her teeth. Continued. "Three at a time. Soap, towels, clean clothes provided. Get moving."

As animals in a circus the first showerees departed alongside their ringmasters, heading in a line towards the sweaty, cramped stage of their performance. Small and poky, more shadowed than lit by cheap yellow fluorescent strip lights, crowded with scratched, dented metal lockers and hanging racks, the performers found themselves picking their way across floors littered with blood stained theatre shoes, surrounded by clothes hanging resentfully from hooks like disembowelled animal carcasses in an abattoir, congregating around an open bin overflowing with discarded masks and hats. Accosted by the aroma of sweat, dirty feet and fungoid infections it was with some relief that the quarantined ones pitched themselves into the adjoining showers, avoiding the toilets. Better to pee in the shower than use one of those. At least the water was warm. The 'soap' was that skin-peeling sanitised hand stuff freely available in any NHS institution but it did the trick and was particularly adept at removing dried vomit. The towels were small, thin affairs but clean and easy to hurl into the already full bin. They fell like clouds around it onto the floor, blending into the dirt with alacrity.

It was the reappearance of the newly bathed in the waiting room that made Dawn decide to act. Devoid of their own clothes which they had been obliged to surrender to the laundry, they were dressed in disposable gowns, made from paper, employed in the operating theatre as sterile protection during surgical procedures.

"I'm not bleeding wearing one of those" she announced and stamped a swollen foot. "No bloody way".

"Sit down and shut up. It is what it is…. Next."

As Tracy, now released from behind her computer and very much part of the crowd was marshalling the next in line for cleaning, Dawn made her move.

Steadily, stealthily, with an agility inspired by wrath she levered herself out of the row of chairs, away from Shazza whose jaw was suspended in mid-air and paddled towards the exit. The double doors saw her approaching and sprang into action, delighted. At last! Something to do! They uncoupled themselves and moved smartly aside. Dawn sailed through, propelled by the momentum of her own girth and fury, bound for freedom.

It should have worked. It would have worked, she later told Shazza, if she'd had that mobility scooter and those interfering, fascist, right wing government puppets had not intercepted her at the tape. She could have walked straight through it – nothing to stop her. The police were no match for her but it was that dreadful paparazzi man that had made it all go wrong. She had no idea where he came from. Hiding in the bushes probably, with his camera, just waiting to pounce on her. Now she knew what it felt like to be Lady Di. There had been a horrible flash – like lightning - and she was blinded so she had to stop. That was when the police had got to her at the same time as the reporter, who only wanted to interview her. It wasn't her fault that they were all now in quarantine as well. Served them right.

This was not entirely true. The journalist, an ambitious young man from the local paper who had his sights set on Canary Wharf and editorship by the time he was thirty had 'seized the day' (or night) as he later wrote.

"Yes! I'm in!" he had hollered into his mobile phone as he was escorted by the police officers also exposed to Dawn as all four made their way back through the double doors into the waiting room.

The presence of a journalist – only the local rag but a reporter nevertheless – impressed the isolated ones. It gave the event a certain gravitas. They were newsworthy! All were exceptionally keen to be interviewed, photographed, emailed out to the world; even Dawn, who insisted on being first, as it was she who had made it possible. He wasn't all bad, she conceded to Shazza after speaking to the young man at such length he had had to escape to the toilet. Only doing his job after all, and they all had a living to earn, didn't they? Graham Parsons was less sanguine.

"What do you mean the Press are here?" he hammered at Kirmani (who really ought to have been an anaesthetist the way he behaved). At least the MD thought it was the ED Consultant – so difficult to tell in those white suits, hats and masks. Graham Parsons was himself similarly garbed but his identity was never in doubt thanks to MEDICAL DIRECTOR written in heavy, black permanent marker which shouted out from his chest and back. He need not have bothered – hospital employees knew who he was because of the way he peered over his glasses and no one else much cared.

The child admitted with suspected meningitis had been moved into isolation with his mother as a precaution. Already in possession of one virus, they were keen not to let him contract another. Sister D. suspected that the mother was quite happy with the arrangement – two weeks away from reality and her estranged husband, all services provided, at no expense to herself. Plenty to watch on her mobile and iPad (she never went anywhere without them) but what about charging cables? This was indeed a problem of increasing anxiety throughout the quarantined ones, all of whom "Absolutely" had to have contact with the outside world.

Reluctantly the Medical Director agreed to arrange a delivery of brand new, unopened, uncontaminated mini-usb cables and harmony was restored. Perhaps the supplier could be persuaded to provide them free of charge as a gesture of good will in such extenuating circumstances? They now had, after all, a resident journalist who could report such an act of generosity … The MD would leave it with the HR manager, now dressed, who heartily wished he would swiftly succumb with something debilitating and leave her alone.

She was not the only one. Tracy, showered and suited in white, piebald hair flattened greasily inside in what looked like a shower cap, her eyes glaring over the mask that moved in and out with speech and breathing, was doing her best to avoid Graham Parsons. He. however, had other ideas.

"We still need to discuss the unfortunate allegations made against you, Miss Spanner" he said, lenses glinting. "Not at this precise moment, obviously, but I will ask my secretary to arrange a suitable time."

"How?" Tracy wordlessly glowered back, mask moving violently with the depth of her breaths.

"She will continue to manage my diary and perform her duties" he answered, "even though she is not on the premises. Thank goodness for modern technology. It will be necessary to liaise with your line manager, of course, in the first instance. Then… well … we'll have to see."

What he did not say, but they both knew, was that this was just the start. The Medical Director would have liked to be discreet but he was a very busy man…and she was only admin.

"Unfortunately, the discussion has become more complicated in the light of some of your other actions this evening Miss Spanner."

Did he mean disarming the knifeman?

"It is most regrettable that due to a failure to follow hospital procedures according to your job description, we all now find ourselves in a very difficult situation with, er, national implications. We are all on the line here, Miss Spanner." Thanks to you, hung in the air.

Then he had moved on, to fry more important fish.

She felt sick. He was blaming her when it was not her fault. None of this was her fault. Nothing she had ever done had been her fault yet she was always the one who paid, who got the blame, ever since she could remember. She hadn't asked her mother to get pregnant or be deserted or be angry.

She wanted to vomit but knew she couldn't. So, she would have to cut herself. There must be something sharp close to hand – this was a hospital for Christ's sake.

As she sagged towards the treatment room, Tracy determined not to answer her phone. Not much need for her desk top and work station either, she was musing… so she would be able to avoid the MD's secretary (poor cow).

Her mobile pinged with a text. Well it couldn't be the secretary, not yet. Tracy eased herself into a corner, away from curiosity and gossip, and opened the text.

It was from Stacey.

"WTF? yru txtn me? Y shud I help u? U deserve everything u get. Mum n dad r right. U got it coming. Blocking u bitch."

Rohan Patel tried to turn over but found himself uncomfortably constrained by untied strings and copious amounts of thin NHS cotton wrapped around his torso. Also, the bed was very hard … and narrow …. and draughty around his legs. Clearly, he was not at home. He eased up his eyelids, blinking against the harsh light and found himself in close encounter with an NHS blue paper curtain, as disposable as himself. … Why was he in a hospital cubicle? In the treatment room? He recognised the curtains. They were moving from side to side and, more unusually, up and down with a nauseating spinning motion that was most unpleasant so he closed his eyes against it. But the spinning continued and then he remembered, mostly because he could taste sour whisky vomit lining his mouth. Lifting his arm to smite his no longer sweaty brow he found it locked by cannula and tube to a drip, now less than half full but still resolutely dribbling its contents into his thirsty person. Groaning he forced himself into a sitting position. His genitalia, pleased to be mobile once more, shifted to one side as his legs were bent up and then flopped back onto the bed out of harm's way as his belly descended onto his thighs. It had been nice to be out in the open, enjoying the view, sharing the light but time now to return to the soft comfort of their hairy darkness. If only he would put on some underpants.

Where was everyone? It had been too easy to help himself to a set of clean, over pressed cardboard stiff scrubs from the linen store in which to affect his escape. Plenty of noise from the staff changing rooms though so he would have to avoid those, male and female, but ample opportunity to find footwear in any of the patient changing rooms in Imaging. It never even entered Rohan's mind that he had been there before that evening as he slipped into one of the small cubicles adjoining the white, sealed room with the CT scanner, but this time he was unlucky. Nothing to find. He would have to go barefoot. Thus it was he plodded flaccidly along increasingly dim, quiet corridors, ready at any moment to detour in the face of oncoming humanity. But no one came. He walked, more confidently – nay strode – away from the hospital thoroughfares into the alleys and backyards of the main building, the parts of the hospital frequented only by lowly support staff, tradesmen, the maintenance department and first year medical students who had not yet found their bearings. And out. Through the narrow side laundry door, into freedom.

Chapter Twelve

The treatment room was quiet and orderly. Fronk, a slight white figure now less anarchic than weedy, was bent over one of the larger members of the closing time crowd. The man had cut his head, or rather his head had been cut – 'not 'is fault mate - the bottle did it'. Dr Mac had wanted to stitch it, the man objected, copious amounts of local anaesthetic and tender loving care were promised, the man agreed, the head was sewn and now Fronk was dressing the wound. Mac was trying to attend to someone with a deep voice and vertiginous female footwear… Tracy could hear the high heels clacking on the floor as the person was escorted to a cubicle, arguing loudly about the nature of the disposable gowns and footwear they were being forced to wear. Those platforms, three-inch heels had cost a fortune; there was no way they were going out for cleaning or recycling or incinerating or whatever they were going to do with other people's private property. Someone might nick them – they were designer – couldn't trust no-one these days – especially in a hospital the voice was saying darkly. Mac was clucking sympathetically but otherwise silent. Tracy heard the curtain swish, the shoes stop, the narrow bed groan and a soft crackle as disposable gown met paper sheet. Then the legs landed on the bed which sighed and there was a sliding rustle as the shoes were removed from the feet.

Yes, Mac did understand. Perhaps if they were put into a sealed bag… and kept sealed, somewhere safe? … Excellent. Now, let's have a look at that rash. Lie back … bend your knees up, legs wide apart… let them flop to the side. …that's it … try to relax…. lovely. … I'm just going to lift this up a bit… Goodness. No wonder you're sore.

No sign of the square with stretched buttocks that was Sister D. so Tracy edged her way further into the room. She still held her mobile but it was turned off, completely, and she gripped it with knuckles as white within latex gloves as her suit. Just another shapeless blob going about hospital business, strangely calm and leisurely now that the portals were sealed. Those that were in, were in, and had all the time in two weeks to be treated. Almost like going private Dawn and Shazza had agreed, apart from the facilities and the food. The food! Oh my God! What would they have to eat for the next fourteen days…not hospital food, surely? They couldn't do that to them; that was inhuman. The final insult, apart from the debacle about finding them something to wear. They simply did not believe that disposable gowns could not be found in their size – it was just sheer bloody-mindedness, someone determined to be difficult and unpleasant – probably that Tracy. Wouldn't put anything past her. Well, something would just have to be found because Dawn (and Shazza, yeah?) was not going to expose any part of her person (ANY of it) in any shower or changing room in the world without suitably modest attire. And if they thought she was using one of those pathetic towels, they could think again. Wouldn't dry so much as a leg; she'd need at least three. Then they'd scratch and she had sensitive skin, she did, had had it all her life, and she was just about fed up to the back teeth with the whole bloody thing. Shazza said she wished she was – she was starving, and they began all over again.

The store room was at the far end of the treatment room. There was a keypad for access but, although she shouldn't, Tracy knew the code – the date of birth of Sister D's predecessor, the one who had left to start a tattoo parlour. Pretty well everyone knew the code that ought to have been changed regularly, in line with senior management security protocols, but then no one would be able to get in because departments never talked to each other. During busy times – and this Saturday night definitely qualified as one of those – the door was discreetly propped open. Not on this occasion though, Tracy noticed. Probably because the police and Medical Director were nosing around. In a way that was better because she could quietly key in the code, pull the door just wide enough to enter then close it behind her. She would have to be quick; the disposable gowns, sheets and curtains were kept in here and someone would be in to stock up or try and find something huge enough for those two mingers in the waiting room.

One disposable scalpel would be enough, but she took two. Just in case. It was easy to slip the slender blister packs into her sleeve where they snuggled above the elastic cuff, the slim blades with their pale blue plastic handles close against the very skin they would soon split apart: sterile, cold, calming, soothing. The question was now, where to go?

Somewhere private, undisturbed, alone. Near a sink so that she could wash afterwards and clear up, but not so far away as to be difficult to return to reality. She was going to say normality but stopped herself - who knew what that was? As she left the treatment room, still quiet, as if it fallen asleep where it stood, she passed a deserted nurse's station. Presumably they had gone with the patients deported from the back of the building. Wherever they were, the colour coded keys used to access everything forbidden and locked away were to be seen, flaunting themselves, winking at her from the desk beside the phone and an almost full tin of Celebrations. At the top of the keys, like an omen, was the one coded white. The Holy Grail: the drugs cupboard. Too good to be true. She helped herself to three Milky Ways which she unwrapped and stuffed under her face mask into her mouth –

who cared about dieting now? - as she picked up the keys and padded towards the white cupboard on the wall. Her head was hammering, her joints ached, the Red Bull had long since worn off and she might need them later, when she could not sleep.

Two blue boxes, labelled Paracetamol, 100 tablets, 10 strips of 10, cuddling together at eye level on the shelf. One opened and half used, the other spare, virginal, untouched: full. Nobody would notice if it went missing. They would just think that the pharmacy assistant (if there even was one at the moment) had not stocked up, and it had been a busy shift, even by Saturday night standards. Paracetamol wasn't a controlled drug – Tracy knew that – how else could she have had so much, so freely, so often if it was? No need to sign it out in duplicate and anyway, who the hell cared? No one ever seemed to care.

It was easy to slide the unopened box into her sleeve. No fingerprints from latex-skinned hands of course, then shut the door, lock it, pad back to the nurse's station and deposit the keys exactly where she had found them, white colour code on top. Help yourself to a couple more chocolates, (Maltesers this time, her second favourite) then melt into the corridor.

If she went back towards the treatment room, she could look for a secluded cubicle or one of the consulting rooms with a sink. Both had beds and chairs so she could choose her vantage point, all the better to cut herself. Probably a bed because of the paper sheets that could be easily discarded easily afterwards. She could hear Mac's Antipodean burr as he chatted amiably to his patient in harmony with the splurt of something from a tube, then the time worn apology that it might feel a bit cold but it'd warm up soon enough. A small gasp from the anointed one because it was effin freezin' mate. Fronk could be heard from behind a blue curtain (why was everything blue? Why not something more cheerful?) speaking very slowly and clearly. He could have been talking to himself for all the response he got but as he was discussing the propensity of toes to turn black and gangrenous as a result of neglected feet in diabetics, it seemed unlikely. Tracy passed on, unnoticed, unheard, hidden in her own mind. It would have to be the arms – below the elbow which was lower down than usual but she did not have much time and the white suit was a real handicap. Better to pull up the sleeves than have to disrobe completely as she would have to do if she wanted to do her thighs. They would have to wait for another time, tingle as they might in anticipation. Anyway, it would be difficult to conceal incisions there in this frickin' suit whereas she could do her arms quickly and efficiently. And it would have to be the left as she was right-handed and doing it the other way around took time and concentration when all she wanted right now was comfort and consolation. A pain she could understand and cope with, to block out all the others. Pain that was self-inflicted and controllable: hers, personal, planned.

That would do! A narrow cubicle, squeezed in like an afterthought at the end of the row, just a bed and a sink. A clean open curtain that could be discreetly pulled across far enough to hide but not so far as to appear fully closed so that anyone passing might think it was an empty space, hastily abandoned. Tracy sidled in and sneaked the paper almost across the opening, thanking the gods that Mac was so chipper and never stopped talking. She could heave herself onto the bed and start to unwrap without being heard. Not that anyone cared to listen. They never did.

The scalpel. So thin, so slender, so light. Like air. So sharp. You never felt it go in and slice the flesh which seemed to unseal of its own accord. No blood at first – that came with the sting and pain that followed. A pain as sharp as the blade at first, then an angry, thudding ache that twisted and turned with time and movement. After a while – a long while, hidden beneath sleeves, it would ease and all that would remain would be an angry raised line of flesh that would eventually turn white, even if the rest was burned brown by sun. She held the light blue handle up to the light and, just for a second, studied the metal blade with awe, anticipating, excited, as a junkie before a fix, longing for escape. Then it happened.

"It's for your own good."

It was a woman's voice. Soft yet cruel, suppressed – wanting to be loud but not daring to because of neighbours, nosy parkers, interfering do-gooders: witnesses.

"Yeah. Do as you're told. We don't want to have to make you."

Now the voice was male. Close by. Tracy began to shake.

****

It was getting dark outside. The kitchen cabinets glowed mustard in the ebbing light and highlighted the smears on the free-standing electric cooker which leered greasily at her as she sat on a high stool at the Formica kitchen table. In front of her was a bowl of rice pudding, plentiful, cold, congealed, the milk-skin over it crinkling and shrinking with every passing hour. On one edge was a shallow indentation, a toe in the water, pitifully small in comparison to what remained. She had put her spoon, initially sticky but now dried and crusty, on the grimy surface beside the bowl and sat, hunched on a harsh wooden stool.

Lunch was a lifetime ago. It had not been a bad meal as meals went, until her mother had slammed the dish down in the centre of the table. Tracy had not spoken, or been spoken to, so had not said anything wrong. Stacey, babbling in her high chair had been attempting to feed herself which had highly entertained her adoring parents who were delighted with the way food had been deposited over chair, hair, face, clothes and audience. No one had taken any notice of the older girl, the wrong-half, sister. Tracy hated rice pudding. All slippery and lumpy at the same time, welded together so that you could not separate it and had to swallow it in a lump, like when you had sick in your mouth and couldn't let it out so you had to make it go back down. She hated milk too – thick fatty sweetness that stuck on the tongue and left a white furry coat that would not go away. She could imagine it tunnelling down her throat leaving a heavy, smelly trail all the way down to her stomach, where it would expand and grow into rancid cottage cheese that would make her feel sick, then it would try to escape and push its way back up again. Her mother deliberately burned the top of the pudding because she liked the black bits, which she took for herself with a kind of ingratiating apology for having the oven too hot, which they all knew was a lie. Then the pale sludge exposed below was slopped into bowls and handed out, with a spoon, to be shovelled down before it gets cold.

Except Tracy could not eat it.

"Would not" her mother said and her step father grunted with disapproval but did not speak because he was too busy eating. Plenty to say when he had finished though. Tracy knew what was coming and tried, she really tried, to block out every sense and to swallow the first spoonful. But she could not do it. Noisy gagging served only to make things worse so now she found herself, ostracised but not alone, sitting at the table 'until you've eaten every last bit' as the day died.

If only someone would save her. Would fly in like Cinderella's fairy godmother, eat the rice pudding, put a cushion on the stool and tell her she could get down from the table. Let her go to her room and pretend she was in someone else's life. Then Monday would come and she could go to school. Not that she was clever or liked school much, but it wasn't home and although she got bullied for being heavy and ginger, no one hit her with a belt like her step-father. Not that she had actually been hit – well, only a few times – but the threat was ever present. He had this way of winding the belt into a tight, curled ball then suddenly flicking it out really fast, like a leather tongue, so that it licked against the table with a crack and a sting that hurt just to hear it. And when he did it her mother always said,

"It's for your own good"

and he always said it was her fault because

"You made me do it".

****

"What do you mean he's gone?"

Sister D. liked to think of herself as both a tolerant and patient (in the healthy sense of the word) person, but really, Fronk was crossing precious boundaries. "He must be there."

"He's not."

"Then where is he?"

A shoulder shrug, a shake of the head and subsequent flap of the ear discs within the elasticated hood like a dog shaking itself dry and Fronk successfully conveyed to his superior that he had absolutely no idea. They were talking about Rohan.

"Show me."

Dog following at heel again, Fronk followed Sister D's square stretched buttocks down the centre of the treatment room towards the cubicle in which she fully expected to find the recovering drunk. The curtain was drawn fully across the entrance so she almost ripped it open knowing with fury that Rohan would be there and that Fronk had either got the wrong cubicle or had somehow had a complete visual aberration. Who could fail to see something the size of Rohan, magnified in volume by such a confined space, fully exposing himself? It was a sight hard to forget; Fronk was an idiot. The holes in his ears seemed to be eating into his brain. And she really did not have time for this.

"He's not there."

Fortunately, she did not see Fronk's smile of vindication. He, after all, was the reason that Rohan had been there in the first place and she had no intention of letting him forget it.

"Find him. He can't have gone far, not without proper clothes and shoes. I told the Medical Director (sniff) that he was my responsibility … even though he is yours." Now she actually deigned to glare at Fronk. "He is to be found and returned, immediately." He might have been a lost parcel or pet for all she cared. Patients, especially suspended members of staff, did not go missing on her watch. Turning with dramatic emphasis and a hearty plastic crackle she obliged Fronk to scuttle aside as she removed herself and her buttocks from the empty cubicle and launched herself back into the treatment room which awoke with a start and stood by its beds.

Chapter Thirteen

Sister D. delegated the search to Fronk. She would assist but it was essential to maintain a steady, calm demeanour so as not to alarm the already belligerent internees of the waiting room. She, therefore, and Mac would continue to organise the treatment of quarantined ones, with the help of Mr Kirmani, of course, (more sniffing) while Fronk found the elusive Rohan and confined him to barracks. The possibility of not finding him was not even considered. He would be there, somewhere – he always was. It was just a matter of smelling him out. Start with the treatment room then widen the search if necessary. He would be found in a hole, or a corner or in a changing room in Imaging Sister D. hissed, gimlet-eyed, judge, jury and jailer. Besides, she had to get back to her patient – an awkward adolescent (distaste twisted her mouth up to her nostrils). The girl needed IV antibiotics but was refusing to let them put in a cannula – didn't like the needle, apparently. She was phobic. It frightened her so much she felt sick and would pass out, die of fright, get PTSD. It would scar and people would think she did drugs and not just weed but the hard stuff and how would she ever live it down?

"I've tried telling her it's for her own good" said she of the stretched buttocks with such severity that Fronk blamed himself, "but she won't listen."

Sister D. was not a person to whom one did not listen.

"I wanted to see if Mac could talk to her – he's good with babies – but he's up to his armpits in lubricant and another anus. We'll probably have to sedate her and that means finding an anaesthetist but they're all tied up in theatre with the cracked chest."

She had only stepped out for a minute and had to get back as soon as possible she said, or the girl's exasperated father was in danger of pinning her down and inserting the needle himself. Which would never do. It was at this point, she glared, that Fronk had told her about Rohan. So, he had better be found, hadn't he? Soon. By the time she had finished with the recalcitrant adolescent.

She steered her bulk smartly around in one movement and pointed herself in the direction of the tiresome teenager, letting momentum and size propel her forwards. Fronk stayed for a moment longer then went the opposite way, peering as professionally as he could behind every curtain, obstacle and impediment as he began his search. Quite why he thought he might find one of Rohan's girth behind a chair or drug's trolley was not evident but at least he would be able to say that he had looked everywhere. Heavy dread in his solar plexus, like congealed rice pudding, was telling him that this would not go well; he had to cover himself.

The stroppy teenager had apparently been told her fortune by her father by the time Sister D. returned and the cannula was duly inserted, with a manageable amount of moaning, groaning, grimacing, sighing, sucking in of breath, eye rolling and mouth tightening. The drip was attached, the antibiotics began to trickle and order was restored. The girl had arranged herself as aesthetically as disposable gowns allowed and her father sat beside her, similarly but less artistically attired, wondering how the hell he was going to manage the next two weeks with his mardy offspring without his wife to share the load. Just like her mother he muttered to himself as he morosely prepared himself for the long haul. Sister D. left them to it.

"Sorry!" Fronk said as the teenager and her father looked up at his white framed face as he squinted in at them. "Wrong cubicle."

He had not found Rohan, nor anything to do with him. The man had vanished. Only a detached drip, a crumpled sheet vaguely compressed into the shape of a recumbent male like a disposable Turin shroud bore witness to the fact that Rohan had ever existed.

"No-one's indispensable" Fronk was philosophising as he moved on to the next cubicle. "Here one minute then gone the next – the waters just close over us, the ripples fade and that's it".

At first, he did not know who it was, lying on its back, hooded head turned away from him, completely white-suited apart from one arm exposed below the elbow. The inelegant elastic cuff had been pushed uncomfortably up the arm and was pressing into the bare flesh which had plumped out around the elastic frill. A mesh of white marks, pink marks and thin open splits, an inch or so long, straight but haphazard, random lines, blade-brush strokes, festooned the arm which was dribbling blood onto the paper. Not in pools or torrents but enough to sink and spread, to soften and soak the absorbent sheet and to shriek colour. A disposable scalpel lay beside the inert body.

Graham Parsons was struggling. The most recent directive from Public Health England requiring all medical personnel and those in protective gear to wear goggles, felt like a final straw. How would he see without his glasses? Or rather, how could he be seen without them? Perhaps he should have one of those perspex helmets? How others whose sight depended on prescription lenses would manage was of no concern; let them sort these things out for themselves. Initiative was absolutely requisite in apocalyptic times of such as these: survival of the most ingenious … and deserving he added to himself, as he wrote his identity in black capital letters on another white suit.

He was not best pleased therefore when it was reported to him that Rohan Patel (who was an anaesthetist) had 'gone missing', 'was nowhere to be found' and it looked very much as if he was not on hospital premises. Not only was an alleged sexual predator on the loose but also one who had breached stringent quarantine restrictions and was even now somewhere unknown, possibly spreading Coronavirus the length and breadth of Wyeminster and even beyond. The man was a menace and, what was worse, appeared to be clad in not one but two NHS gowns marked as the property of the Wyeminster NHS Trust. He was therefore instantly traceable back to the hospital and the auspices of its Medical Director, Graham Parsons. Added to which, the police had been in touch. They had identified the knifeman and wanted to know if the hospital had any record of him. Apparently, he had asserted that he knew the hospital, had often been there, that they knew him and it was all part of The Plan. The Voices had told him to do it. He had tried to resist – had washed his hair repeatedly with anti-dandruff shampoo to get rid of them but it had not worked. Not even when he was washing his hair right outside the hospital. The Voices would not go away, despite the fact that he took off all his clothes and rinsed himself in the rain which was clean water, not like that poisonous stuff They sent through the taps. They spoke through taps. That was why he was refusing to shower. He had even heard Them in the street lights at night which was why he put silver foil over his head under his hat when he went outside. They had very kindly accompanied him to the twenty-four/seven supermarket to buy the knife with which to defend himself and guided him to the right section. (There were so many aisles). Without Their help he would have been quite lost but They had recommended a smooth carving knife rather than anything serrated – better for slicing. The police also wanted to know if he had a history of drug abuse. He had tested positive for marijuana which was known to trigger 'episodes' in paranoid schizophrenics.

What on earth was a Medical Director supposed to do to assist with such banalities in the early hours of a viral lockdown on a Sunday morning? Mr Parsons wanted to know. His secretary would follow it up for them but, in the meantime, they would just have to wait and keep the man in isolation, as much for their own safety as his. Had they contacted the local psychiatric unit? … Then perhaps they should. Non-clinicians were so easily confused about medical institutions. Which was understandable, of course, without the proper medical training but nevertheless made things so much more complicated for the medical professionals. To be honest, he was surprised that the police had contacted him but no, he was happy to help, even if he was exceptionally busy. Always happy to help. Just call his secretary.

"It's Tracy." Fronk was working on stemming the flow from the cuts on her arm, one of which was perilously close to the artery in her wrist. He was grasping them, hard, trying to apply enough pressure to stop the bleeding. "They need stitching. She's used a scalpel and gone deep." Sister D. had just arrived, wrenching open the curtain in her haste; it wriggled indignantly but held, just long enough to be accosted by Mac's arrival as he was removing one set of latex gloves in order to don another. Hopefully not another rectum was his first thought.

"What's happened?" was his second as he spoke from the doorway.

Fronk was turning Tracy's head over to face them. It flopped into position, hard and heavy, so white that it had begun to blend in with her hood. Blood pooling unevenly over her white waterproof suit had begun to trickle into its creases and folds before it headed for the paper sheet and then, when that could take no more, onto the floor.

"Hell!" Mac said by way of an answer and pushed past Sister D to examine the arm that Fronk was grimly squeezing.

"It looks like she's done this before ... Let's see the other one."

Yes, similar scars and marks on her right arm, the only difference being that there were less of them.

"Cut the sleeves, quickly, so that I can suture ... thanks, Fronk. ..."

He did not need to say more. All three were appalled at the sight of the upper arms, striated and discoloured, bearing testament to systematic self-harming over what had to have been a long, long time judging by the various shades of red, pink, white and raised flesh. And they had not even seen her thighs.

"I had no idea." Sister D said softly.

Fronk shook his head in agreement and resisted the urge to cry so he pulled at his ear lobes but could not find them in the hood of his Hazmat suit.

Mac had taken control. No time to lose. Fronk took blood for testing and cross matching, set up a drip then blood pressure and vital signs were to be closely monitored; she was completely out of it. The blister pack in which the scalpel had come was there and a second scalpel, unused. At least they were sterile Mac mused, but no one smiled. They had to stop the bleeding, give her time to recover then address the issue of self-harming. Thankfully there was no urgent need for a waiting room receptionist at the moment so she could be left in peace. Stitched, wounds dressed and asleep, the curtain across the cubicle was respectfully (to its relief) pulled shut so that Tracy's indignity remained private; not quite her own property now but in safe hands.

"What is it?"

Dawn was struggling; visibly distressed. How much more could she take?

"I can't eat that." She shook her head sadly and her chins wobbled sympathetically in an attempt to console and comfort. "Whatever it is."

Shazza was examining the package on her own lap.

"I think it's a sandwich." She looked more closely, bending down as far as possible but carefully refraining from touching it, just in case. Encased in its non-recyclable plastic sheath the sandwich – for such it once was – stared back at her. It was difficult to see clearly through the greasy plastic but the oil smeared writing on the cardboard inner at the back claimed that one was ham and the other cheese. Together a happy pairing promising taste, variety and satisfaction but separately, suffocated within limp white bread, compressed like foam rubber lined with a magnolia film of fat purporting to be butter, they made an unhappy couple. Divorced but not separated, forced to cohabit without compatibility or compromise. The sallow cheese lay thin, processed and without flavour inside the bread. The ham, for such the even thinner watery pink slime-line claimed to be, had clearly given up all hope of savour, lain down and died, without so much as a smear of mustard to mourn its passing. No seasoning, or pickle or even the slimmest of slim slices of tomato to relieve the pain. Dawn was in torment.

"I can't eat that" she repeated, with the finality of a Roman emperor giving the thumbs down to a dying gladiator in the Coliseum. "Something's gotta be done."

Every head in the waiting room jerked up and listened. Presented with similarly tragic culinary offerings, they too were in doubt. One or two of the more intrepid had peeled back the plastic to unveil the contents within but no one had actually eaten any part of them. The journalist however, was enthusiastically taking close ups of the comestibles on his mobile and emailing them straight back to base. NHS food always made a great headline; so much scope for puns and cheap jibes. If only he could come up with something memorable, the stuff that catchphrases are made of, worthy even of that arbiter of all things headline, *The Sun*. Thumb Man had taken the precaution of using his now dressed digit for a safer tactile examination of the article. The offerings were, according to the Hazmatted Being who had distributed them, 'left overs'. Quite what from or, more significantly, when, had not been specified.

Dawn lifted herself magnificently out of her seat and settled her weight.

"I want someone in authority" she declared, adjusting her paper clothing as if it was ermine. Her feet began to twitch, to move, to shuffle, her ankles followed with her calves close behind and then her whole body. She was on the move.

"Where're you going?" Shazza asked for all of them.

"To get someone." Ominous, dark, a storm gathering, she billowed forth in the direction of the treatment room. "No sign of that Tracy – typical – so I'll just have to find someone to get this sorted. I'm starving."

Sister D. was the unlucky recipient. Dawn found her almost immediately on the other side of the door which was lucky, as she was about to faint with hunger and if not provided with adequate nourishment would almost certainly collapse and be in need of urgent medical treatment, so Sister Whatever She Called Herself had better organise something soon, hadn't she? At which point the famished one swayed a little, put her hand to her brow and sighed from the depths of her stomach.

Sister D was unimpressed and even more unhelpful. They had been given all that was available; it was short notice, the weekend, the hospital was in lockdown and they were lucky to have got anything at all. No, coffee and tea were not freely available but there was plenty of water in the cooler. It wasn't her fault if the vending machine was empty or they had run out of money; this was the NHS, not the Ritz. It was what it was, but she could assure her that things would be sorted out in time. No, she did not know at exactly what time, that was not what she had meant.

Then why had she said it Dawn wanted to know and folded her arms over her chest. Why say something you don't know the answer to? There were a lot of very hungry people out there (she indicated the waiting room with a disdainful flick of her head) and kept her arms crossed, armour-like. Bring it on they seemed to say.

Christopher Reeve as Superman could not have made a timelier arrival than Mr Kirmani who, at that moment, appeared on the scene.

"Can I help, ladies?" he asked, having recognised the stretched buttocks in the white plastic and unable to misinterpret Dawn's bosom even though he had only seen it once before entwined with a green man and a disability scooter.

"Yes" they answered together but Dawn managed to prevail.

"And you are?"

"Mr Kirmani. Emergency Department Consultant."

"Well, Mr Kirmani…" and she was off.

The consultant heard and understood, every word. He really did. Of course, a proper meal was required and indeed, would be, just as soon as it could be organised. He fully accepted that the hospital was responsible for feeding its er, clientele, and he would ensure that that responsibility was fulfilled. Meanwhile, he and Sister Rees had a patient who required urgent attention so he was sure that she … Dawn, thank you; that Dawn would understand and that she would also be kind enough to explain to those in the waiting room? Thank you, Dawn. Very much appreciated and he steered himself and the stretched buttocks down the room towards Tracy.

Dawn performed a most impressive about turn in limited space and headed back from whence she came.

"What happened?" Shazza asked as her friend filled the doorway.

"Pass us your phone, Shazza. Mine's flat."

"I haven't got much battery. They've promised us chargers but I don't know when."

Dawn sniffed, much as Sister D might.

"Enough for what I want…" She was already tapping a familiar number on the screen.

"Who're you calling?"

"Ssh. I need to concentrate. ... Right."

She addressed the room.

"What do you all want to eat?"

Dawn did an admirable job of assimilating, filtering, disseminating and tapping on the screen exactly what was required. The journalist was astonished; perhaps he had underestimated her. Size wasn't everything. Besides, he was hungry too. It had been ages since the kebab when the pub closed but he, even he, known to eat complete crap when in pursuit of a story or even to go without food altogether (alcohol was a marvellous appetite suppressant), had drawn a line at the sandwiches. There were depths below which even the Press refused to go. The call took longer than Shazza would have liked in terms of battery life but on the other hand, she was getting a substantial repast and so, it seemed, was everyone else.

"I think that's it…" Dawn said, eventually, looking round at the heads bobbing up and down like ducks on a choppy pond. In the box for special instructions she wrote that she knew it was a big order but they'd be quick, yeah? Everyone was starving. Delivery to the main entrance but no contact. As for remuneration, she hit the Payment on Delivery option and pressed send.

"The hospital'll pay" she announced to her audience. "Mr Kirmani said so. He's the Emergency Department Consultant and says he's happy to accept responsibility. We're his clients."

"How was she when you first saw her?"

"The same, without suturing of course."

"Has she come around at all?"

Sister D. nodded. "Yes, but only briefly. She was very confused and agitated as well as drowsy. We couldn't get any sense out of her. To be honest, I thought she might be drunk but she clearly isn't." Not like some I could mention her sniff said.

"Has she vomited?"

"Not that I'm aware of."

"She's not responding. She should be more alert than this by now – waking up, showing signs of recovery…. Let's do more bloods, including liver function. Are we sure she hasn't done anything, taken anything in addition to the cutting? … Pills?"

"Not as far as I know but I'll call Fronk. He's the one who found her."

"Self-harmers aren't usually suicidal, not unless there are other issues. What do we know about Tracy?" Mr Kirmani stopped…. Then spoke,

"The allegations."

"The Coronavirus won't have helped"

No, it wouldn't. Had someone said something to her? Mr Kirmani and the Sister both thought they knew very well who might. And why. Scapegoat Syndrome as it was known.

Fronk could throw no further light on the situation. Had there been anything else other than the blue handled scalpels? No, not that Fronk had noticed but then he hadn't been looking. At this stage in his shift his mascara had lost its lustre and volume so no, his vision was not impaired and there was nothing. Nothing on the floor? In the sink? No, nothing. Not enough room to swing a kitten so it was hardly possible to hide or lose any evidence other than the empty scalpel blister pack and the unused blade, both of which they already had.

"She's obviously been in the Stores. We need to check and see what else is missing" Mr Kirmani surmised.

Sister D. was already on her way.

"And the drugs trolleys, and cupboards" Mr Kirmani shouted after her. "God alone knows what she might have taken. Is she on any medication, Fronk, do you know?"

"Loads. But all over the counter stuff for aches, pains, migraine, acid stomach, that sort of thing. And Red Bull and coffee."

"Just like the rest of us then. Anything in her handbag or at the desk? We're going to need her medical records, history, the lot. Are you sure there was nothing else here? Anything?"

No, Fronk was absolutely sure. Tracy was as he had found her apart from the fact that he had turned her head to face them.

"She hasn't been moved? At all?"

No, she hadn't. Should they move her now? Change the paper beneath her, maybe move her somewhere more comfortable, a bigger room? No, they would leave her where she was until they had a better idea what was happening but yes, let's change the sheet.

"I'll lift and you pull."

"Christ!"

Lying on the bed, blood soaked, squashed but still recognisable, was an empty packet of paracetamol with ten blister packs of ten, all opened and empty. Their untidy plastic imprint was pressed firmly into Tracy's plastic-covered back and the wet paper that was starting to disintegrate as she was moved.

"She can't have taken them all?" Fronk was horrified. "Not the whole lot?"

"The receptionist? Tracy Spanner? The one who's accused of negligence?" Graham Parsons could not believe that anyone could be so stupid. "When did this happen?"

"That's what we're trying to work out. Not long ago, obviously, but it's a question of finding out whoever saw her last and when, and what kind of frame of mind she was in."

"I bumped into her in the corridor just before the knifeman was disarmed, if that helps."

Kirmani did not look surprised, which was irritating, but then that was the nature of the man, his superior decided.

"How did she seem to you?"

"Fine. I don't know her very well, of course, but she seemed quite normal."

"Did she say anything?"

The Medical Director shook his head. "No, not really."

"That doesn't sound like Tracy. Was she preoccupied would you say?"

Could it be that he, the Wyeminster Trust Medical Director, was being interrogated? By an Emergency Department Consultant? Graham Parsons decided to be charming.

"It's hard to say. But she has got rather a lot on her plate so, yes, perhaps. She knew that the allegations made by Mrs Lewinski against her would have to be investigated, not to mention her role in the current outbreak of Coronavirus. I imagine these were weighing heavily on her mind….and she clearly has a history of mental instability if what you say is true about evidence of previous self-harming. It concerns me that we knew nothing about this."

"We could've helped her."

"Yes." That was not quite what he had meant, but the Medical Director nodded agreeably. His prime concern had been the employment of such an emotional wreck as a frontline representative of the hospital, in a stressful environment that she was clearly ill equipped to handle. As a result, he had a possible legal case and the beginnings of a pandemic to deal with.

"What happens to her now?" he asked, as solicitously as he knew how. Fortunately, it was difficult to read his face through goggles.

"It's almost certainly a massive paracetamol overdose. One hundred tablets, probably on an empty stomach. We've sent off blood for testing paracetamol levels but that takes time, especially in the current circumstances… and the fact that we have had to send it to another hospital as part of the cost cutting exercise that was introduced a couple of months ago. Added to which, in the light of our, er, current lockdown, they are reluctant to do the testing … they're not sure what the protocol is, as there's no precedent. We've administered NAC – N-acetylcysteine" he explained for the benefit of a rheumatologist who demonstrated that he knew perfectly well what it was, thank you, before returning to the issue of the blood test.

"Well, they have to analyse it, obviously. But our priority must, of course, be testing, controlling and monitoring Coronavirus. Is she a cause for concern?"

"Yes. Progressive rising blood lactate and decreasing urine output. She needs to be transferred to a liver unit."

The Medical Director studied the Consultant, remembering only when it was too late that he could not adjust his glasses. He made as if to wipe his goggles.

"Well, of course she must be treated as you think appropriate. What about isolation? She's possibly the greatest potential threat of infection we have at the moment, apart from the contaminated patient, having been so close to him. Have you sent the viral swab?"

Mr Kirmani paused, recovered himself, answered.

"Of course we have but at the moment the turn-around speed is hardly Formula 1. She will be isolated … of course … but 'our priority' must be to transfer her to a specialist unit … or there may not be anything to isolate."

He turned and moved away in the opposite direction, reminding himself that physical violence against members of staff in NHS institutions – even by other members of staff - would not be tolerated and invariably resulted in criminal prosecution.

Tracy was once more unresponsive, immobile and ashen. Only the recently lacerated arm was on display, colourless flesh interspersed with lines of tidy stitches, Mac's best work. Fronk was squeezed on one side the of the narrow bed alongside the monitor; he had just taken her blood pressure and was not happy.

"Low and dropping" he answered the consultant's unasked question as soon as he reappeared in the cubicle, a little flustered but more concerned. They both studied the body.

"We need an intensive care review. I'm concerned about her ability to protect her airway. She's probably heading towards intubation and ventilation."

"What time is it?"

"Just off 5.40."

"Right. Team brief in the staff room at 6.00"

"So much for the Coronavirus update. Now. Tracy." The team looked at each other then back at Mr Kirmani who continued, somewhat subdued. "It looks as if she's ingested 100 tablets."

He spoke through the gasps.

"We're still waiting for the paracetamol levels in her blood to come back - thanks Wyeminster for introducing another cost-cutting initiative - but with a 5 to 6 hour post-ingestion period there is almost certainly going to be significant liver damage. Urine output is tailing off which indicates the need for renal replacement therapy and a large double lumen filtration catheter into her femoral vein. She's already got an arterial line in her wrist – the uncut one – and a Swan Ganz catheter in her neck but she needs to be transferred to a liver unit – Midlands Central. She meets King's criteria, scores 3 for encephalopathy hence the intubation, serum Ph below 7.3 and creatinine above 300. Lactate is above 3.5 but she's not quite had the 4 hours fluid resuscitation."

No one spoke.

"The hepatologist and I are going to have discuss – at some length I imagine – the impact of Covid 19: her risks, the risks of transmission and infection at the receiving centre. We also need to find out more about her physical and especially her mental health. Sister, can you get onto that? Start with her GP."

Long night turning into day, but no end to the darkness.

Chapter Fourteen

Tracy's GP files did little to reassure. Sister D had a quick look at them on screen before forwarding them to Mr Kirmani who secreted himself in an empty consulting room to read them undisturbed: isolation within isolation. The silence was bliss; the reading matter was not. Tracy's records revealed a history of never-ending complaints, illnesses and disorders which could arguably be attributed more to a state of mind than physical sources. It was a wonder she was not addicted to prescription pills: anti-depressants in particular. She seemed to have tried them all over an extended period dating from her teens. What was more alarming was the complete absence of psychological/psychiatric analysis, medical reviews and continuity of care. She had seen every doctor, nurse practitioner and locum her GP surgery had ever had, never the same one twice in succession and sported a record of repeat prescriptions that rolled down the screen like film credits. There was no mention of her self-harming.

According to the hospital employment records her next of kin was a sister, Stacey Spanner. No mention of a partner or parents. It seemed that Tracy led a discreet life, inconspicuous to the point of obscurity. They knew absolutely nothing about her Mr Kirmani realised. Someone they saw every working day (or night), who checked in the out-patients that they met and treated, who was always there, the first point of personal contact for almost all those that were in enough pain or distress to get themselves to A&E, but about whom they knew zilch. Nada. The first thing to do then, was to find out more about her. A psychiatric assessment of her mental state was going to be required but that would not be possible without personal information, an idea of her life, her background, her history. He picked up a landline and rang the contact number on the form.

To his surprise the phone was answered. He had been expecting to leave a message; it was very early on a Sunday morning after all and people with sense and a normal life would still be in bed. Somewhat thrown he introduced himself and asked to speak to Stacey Spanner. It was about her sister, Tracy and he was calling her, the designated next of kin, as a matter of urgency.

"Is she dead?" asked the voice at the end of the phone.

Mr Kirmani was discombobulated, but everyone reacted differently to bad news and it was helpful to be able to get to the point. No, he was very happy to reassure Stacey that Tracy was not dead but he was afraid that she had taken an overdose and that her health was now giving serious cause for concern. They feared that her liver was severely damaged and were planning to have her transferred to a specialist liver centre for treatment. He was extremely sorry to be the bearer of bad news but they had had no choice but to consult her in her capacity as the next of kin; Tracy herself was unconscious and unable to make any decisions or give consent.

"Silly cow. That's just the sort of stunt she'd pull. Full of crap like that she is. Always has been…. whaddya expect me to do?"

"Er…well, as her next of kin we wanted you to be aware of what was happening."

"D'you need my consent or something?"

"No, Tracy is being treated under what's called her best interests but we generally like to have the next of kin on board with any decisions that are made."

"Yeah. That's fine. Whatever."

This was not quite the reaction the consultant was expecting. Oh well, at least there was no hysterical grief to deal with. He moved the conversation on before Stacey drew it to a close as he rather suspected she was keen to do. Perhaps she was in the middle of something?

"It would be helpful to know a little more about Tracy as a person – her background, medical history, that sort of thing. So that we can make informed decisions. Has she for example, ever attempted to take her own life before? Has she ever had any mental health problems?"

"Yeah. Loads. She's a head case. She cuts herself y'know?"

Yes, they did know.

"Done it for years. Always doing that sort of stuff she was. She'd do anything for attention. Always whinging and complaining, throwing herself about. She was a right mardy mare I can tell you. Even called the police on my mum once. The day they chucked her out was a bloody relief."

"They?"

"Mum and Dad but he's not her real dad, he's mine. She's only my half-sister, thank God. None of us have had much to do with her but…oh yeah, she texted me, just last night. That's the first I've heard from her in ages… What about? Some trouble at work – negligence or something. I work at a solicitor's so it was free legal advice what she wanted …. Help her? No, I frickin' didn't. Why would I? What's she ever done for me?"

It was not an edifying account but Mr Kirmani was beginning to get a much clearer idea of Tracy's mental state. Depressing as it was, he persevered. So, it was fair to assume that her relationship with her mother and step father had been rather difficult?

"Difficult? Bloody understatement. Frickin' nightmare. She just never fitted in, know what I mean? And she was jealous of me – so jealous, it used to eat her up. I can't help it that I'm a looker and clever– I got GCSEs and know all about the law. And talking of eating, God, she never stopped – no wonder she was fat and spotty. Always in the fridge she was, even though we all told her how big she was she never took no notice. Tracy's like that –

does just what she wants; never thinks about anybody else. Selfish cow. What did she do? Cut her wrists? Overdose on chocolate and crisps?"

"Paracetamol actually. 100 tablets."

"Shit…. Will she die?" Stacey was taken aback – not to the point of shock but for once Tracy had exceeded even her expectations.

"I hope not. We will do everything we can to restore her back to health. Thank you for your help. I'm afraid it isn't possible to let you see Tracy at the moment – if that's what you wanted -as she's in quarantine for Coronavirus, which I'm sure you know all about. We will, of course, keep you informed about her progress." Not much else to be said, he thought as he put the phone down, except that it was a miracle she hadn't tried to top herself long before.

It was most regrettable, but they had come to the unfortunate conclusion that Rohan Patel was absolutely not on the premises. Anywhere. Yes, they had looked, high and low, as well as deep, shallow, locked, open and behind every door marked strictly private Mr Kirmani added for emphasis, but Graham Parsons was not impressed.

"Regrettable indeed" was all he said and narrowed already slit like eyes to scalpel thin gashes behind his protective goggles. "He must be found. The police will have to be involved. I shall have to inform them about this er, 'unfortunate' situation and I will tell them to liaise with you, Kirmani, should it be necessary in the pursuit of their enquiries. Obviously, the man will have to be traced, apprehended and isolated. He's a threat." Whether this was for carrying a highly contagious infectious disease or because of his alleged sexual predilections was not clear and Mr Kirmani decided not to pursue the matter. Anyway, he did not have the chance. Graham Parsons had other things to discuss, time was of the essence and he was an extremely busy man.

"What's the situation with the overdose?"

"Tracy you mean?"

"Of course. Unless there's another?"

No, no other. Just Tracy. Their Tracy.

"It's definitely a paracetamol overdose – she took the lot and her condition is critical. Midlands Central have agreed that, after a great deal of discussion between myself, their hepatologist, virologist, someone at PHE who had no idea what we were talking about, their Medical Director and a surgeon, they have to take her and she'll almost certainly have to be put on the urgent transplant list. However, there are conditions."

"Conditions?"

"They'll send a helicopter and a transfer team but there are complications because of the virus and the risk of infection. Quite rightly, they have to take extreme precautions. A&E is going to have to be completely cleared so that they have safe points of entry and exit and she'll be air lifted inside a mobile isolation tent."

"That sounds reasonable enough."

It was, the consultant agreed, but the issue was, what to do with everyone currently encamped in the waiting room and treatment area? They had to go somewhere. Had accommodation been arranged yet? Recently emptied wards perhaps? There had also been a … he chose his words with care … 'slight problem' about what they were being given to eat. No transfer of Tracy, which was urgent, could take place until those in quarantine had been catered for. Literally. A mental image of Dawn momentarily blocked out the light and Mr Kirmani shivered. Then his mobile rang.

In the waiting room the air of expectation, spiced with hunger, was as contagious as any virus. Dawn was, literally, "starving". So too it transpired, was everyone else, particularly at the prospect of a proper blow out at someone else's expense although, as Shazza pointed out, in a way they were actually paying for it because they paid taxes which went to pay for the NHS and it was the hospital, which was part of the NHS, and that was going to be paying for the takeaways, so, in a way, they'd paid for it really after all, hadn't they? However, by the time she had reached the *dénouement* of her hypothesis no one was listening, partly because they had no idea what she was talking about but mostly because a fleet of mopeds had been spotted cruising up the concourse towards the main entrance.

A heavenly host descending from on high could not have made a more glorious sight than that procession of mopeds. No despatch rider, messenger, emergency service or divine visitation could have more gladdened the beating hearts and chuntering stomachs of the starving than that line of helmeted riders and their precious cargo. Salvation; sustenance riding pillion in sealed containers, boxes of delights on two wheels. It was a sight to behold. The double doors, so firmly shut and fearing themselves locked down forever brightened their glass, rubbed their draught-proof seal, winked at the lights sprinkled inside the canopy framing their good selves and prepared for action. Any moment now; just like old times.

A brief consultation within the waiting room to elect a representative to receive the goods, the Man with the Thumb and Dawn, naturally, as their self-appointed leader were duly appointed and started to make their way to the isolated side of the doors in anticipation of the heavenly manna to be deposited on the other. Thumb Man appeared to be fully recovered; his injury had been treated and was 'quite comfortable thanks' inside its cosy sterile dressing. No danger of it catching Coronavirus and yes, he was wearing latex gloves so their food would be fine. Anyway, weren't they all in this together? Tracking and documenting every step was their very own member of The Press. So thrilling! Immortality in print! Such a lovely shot of Dawn standing at the doors greeting dawn itself as it sidled coyly from behind the night, a rosy glow, promising warmth, light and a fast food gorge-fest.

Not quite. The Hungry Ones had forgotten to factor the police cordon into their calculations. The Uber Eats delivery fleet had certainly not foreseen such an impediment and had come to an untimely halt, *en masse*, their forces backing up along the concourse like angry wasps mechanically humming. No. They were not getting through. The police had a job to do and they were bleeding well going to do it. No one crossed the tape without authorisation. They did not care if it was an important order, the food would go cold, the recipients were starving, that there would be no contact. Orders were orders. Viruses were viruses and everyone was at risk. It was more than their jobs were worth; they were serving the general public; protecting the health and safety of society. Besides, no one ever thought of them going hungry and thirsty, getting cold, wet, tired and at risk on the front line when they were on duty. No one was getting through. Not if they stayed there all day and night.

Dawn and Thumb Man watched the silent drama unfolding at close hand from behind the glass of the sound proofed doors, which were in a quandary. To open or not to open? All they wanted to do was to oblige, keep all parties happy, fulfil their obligations but it was so difficult to know what to do. On their inside Dawn was shouting and banging the fleshy palm of her hand on their glass at the police, who were completely ignoring her. They in turn were trying hard to be heard over the shouting of the Uber Eats men and began shouting themselves. The mopeds were stationary but their engines were throbbing with fury as they all bent over slightly to one side, perilously balanced by only one foot apiece on the ground, ready to resume equilibrium and surge forward at any moment. The food must get through. They knew it, Dawn knew it, everyone in the waiting room knew it. Even the bandaged digit on Thumb Man's hand knew it and it could not even see what was happening. Mr Kirmani, however, had other ideas.

The relief of being to be able to turn away from his Great Leader and take a phone call was short lived. He was sorry but perhaps he had misheard, why was he being called to the waiting room? Uber Eats? He'd never heard of them. Yes, of course he was the ED Consultant and yes, he did have responsibility for the whole department, but what was this all about? The silence that followed as he listened became heavy, loaded and tight – it chafed. Mr Kirmani's eyebrows rose, bristled, then forged across his brow to meet above the bridge of his nose in scandalised solidarity.

"How much?" he squealed. "Is this a joke?"

Certainly not! It was deadly serious. Now, even now, the food was about to be delivered to the door and payment was required. It was his department, his order, his responsibility. Hadn't he just said so? Payment on delivery is what Uber Eats had been told and that's what they expected.

He arrived at the back of the waiting room at the exact moment that the helicopter, glowing redder and redder in the increasing light, appeared in the sky. With the consultant came others – Fronk, Sister D, Mac, an assortment of nurses, support staff, someone from the kitchen and several porters, including Kolya, who could probably have cleared the room on his own if required. Tracy was with them, unconscious, isolated, on a stretcher within a see-through plastic tent, the access vents for gloved hands sealed up and the whole thing adorned by drips, a ventilator pipe and other medical paraphernalia exiting the top like overgrown vines. The technology at the other end of the pipes was being wheeled alongside the stretcher as closely as an electronic tag on an ankle. Snow White lay in her plastic-glass casket; not a half-eaten apple by her side but the story of a scalpel meeting flesh on her arms. Her full-sized retinue travelled with her. Their mission was to empty the waiting room. The incumbents were to be escorted to makeshift accommodation elsewhere in the hospital. Quite where was, as yet, undetermined, but all that mattered now was to get them out of the way so that Tracy could be safely handed over to her prince in the unlikely form of the transfer team. The young journalist, on his knees at Dawn's feet beside the doors in pursuit of a more artistic shot, barely escaped with his life as for the second time that night, Dawn lost her balance, stumbled, wavered and all but fell upon him so shocked was she by the untimely medical intrusion.

The helicopter circled uncertainly for a few minutes over the confusion of the Uber Eats delivery fleet and the police, standing firm beside their white and blue tape. Its howling and blowing had the effect of scattering the gathered hordes like a sudden breeze through swarming mosquitoes. The only thing to stand firm was Mr Kirmani, adamant that he would not pay for the food. He did not care that they were hungry, that the food might go cold, that it could be handed over without any form of human contact, assuming that the police consented to let it through the cordon. Or even that it had been ordered by Dawn. He was not paying. To a wheel, the mopeds turned and buzzed away, taking their culinary treasures with them.

Dawn's distress was heart breaking. She watched first in disbelief then undisguised anguish as her repast turned tail and disappeared down the concourse, vanishing rapidly into the morning light. It was pitiful. Thumb Man was moved; he clasped her hand with his good one and offered what consolation he could. As they were shuttled away from the doors into the recesses of the hospital, she could be seen still clinging to him as his other hand, injury notwithstanding, edged its way around what he thought might be her waist. The last to leave was the journalist, bereft and forlorn, backing out of the room as a disgraced minion from a royal presence. He would have crawled on his belly not to be banished, to be reprieved, to be allowed to stay. Two weeks with these people? With Dawn? What had he done?

Outside the helicopter had focussed in on the huge yellow 'H' in the cleared area of the car park where it was to land and was descending from the sky, shivering as it approached ground but holding steady. The blades whistled and screamed at the air to move aside, pushing it into wild, wide circles. The grass fringing the parking bays began to dance and twist with short stemmed fury, bending flat to avoid being swept away. This is almost as bad as those sit-on lawn mowers in the summertime it was shrieking, unheard, as the helicopter finally shuddered onto the tarmac while its blades scythed and slashed.

The transfer team were taking no chances. Two paramedics, an anaesthetist, doctor and specialist nurse, bent double like old sacks, Hazmat white, indistinguishable, led the foray into the forbidden land. The double doors were ready, *en garde*. They swung apart on cue, happy to help. This was not just a job; it was a vocation. Their glass glowed red with pride in the reflected light of the helicopter and the emerging morning as they admitted the advancing cavalry. Then they stood back as Tracy – their Tracy –

was wheeled through into the outer world; a world they saw every day but never entered. The blue and white tape had been untied and removed; the police officers stood back, attentive, sombre as a guard of honour at the passing of a funeral cortege. The Hazmatted inhabitants of the Wyeminster stood at the entrance to their abode, framed in the doorway to watch as the paramedics wheeled Tracy to the helicopter where she was loaded into the fuselage with the doctor, the nurse and her technological entourage. A slight altercation was seen to break out. Both paramedics clearly wished to travel with the patient but space was limited so one of them would have to travel up front. They were seen – but not heard – to argue about this until one of them slammed his capacious bag into the front compartment and then to grumpily follow it while his colleague triumphantly leapt into the fuselage.

All this was played out as some kind of macabre tableau against the relentless backdrop of the noisy blades that never got tired. Then another contretemps was seen to commence. The pilot was clearly an unhappy man. He alone was not dressed in protective clothing and, although everyone around him was sealed behind virus-free apparel, he appeared to be protesting about his cargo. How was he supposed to fly wearing a Hazmat suit? He was a pilot not a medic so why should he be exposed to infection? And not just infection, but Covid 19? Why had he not been told beforehand? He would have something to say about this when they got back, they could be sure of that. It was outrageous. An animated discussion involving a great deal of arm waving and gesticulation with the anaesthetist and paramedic relegated to the front ensued; the spectators from the main entrance watched with increasing consternation. Tracy was urgent; she needed to go.

Finally, a lifetime later, the blades picked up speed and blended into one. The helicopter let go of the ground, wobbled, shivered from nose to tail then rose up into the air as a vibrating red bird on a thermal Every head in the doorway was raised heavenwards, following its ascent until it melted into the early morning light and vanished.

Epilogue

"Fronk. Have you got a minute?"

"Not really but for you, anything."

Sister D was bent over the desk at the nurses' station squinting at a computer screen. She was out of her comfort zone and knew it. So did Fronk but neither would ever admit it.

"Just have a look at this for me, will you? How does it read?"

Fronk leant over her white infection-proof plastic-coated shoulder and focussed on the screen. He found himself looking at a job advert.

'A vacancy has arisen at the Wyeminster NHS Hospital Trust for a temporary full-time receptionist for a busy Emergency Department with immediate effect. The successful applicant must be computer literate, personable, a team player and able to cope with sometimes stressful situations. Training will be given. Weekend and night shift work may be required.

For further details and to submit an application, please contact Sister D. Rees (details below). Wyeminster NHS Trust is an Equal Opportunities Employer and an Investor in People, working with the best, for the best, in every aspect of patient care.'

Acknowledgements

We both owe so much to so many. Thank you.
Huge thanks are due, as ever, to our wonderful families: Fiona, Jack, George and Doug for Simon; Nick, Lucy, Pippa, James, Alexis, Alipops, Shirley and Ian for Fionn.
Thank you to all those who have advised, proof read, commented and encouraged, especially Julie, Jenna, Jo, Binks, Chris, Shayna, Jo, Estelle, Lynne.
And very special thanks to Simon, without whom Fionn would not be here and to Fionn, from Simon, for helping keep him sane.

Printed in Great Britain
by Amazon

37809764R00108